winter evenings

By the same author

winter evenings

~ STORIES ~

NAVTEJ SARNA

Navtej Sarna
JLF 2019
Belfast.

RAINLIGHT

RUPA

First published in 2012
in RAINLIGHT by Rupa Publications India Pvt. Ltd.
7/16, Ansari Road, Daryaganj
New Delhi 110002

Sales Centres:

Allahabad Bengaluru Chennai
Hyderabad Jaipur Kathmandu
Kolkata Mumbai

ISBN: 978-81-291-2047-2

10 9 8 7 6 5 4 3 2 1

Navtej Sarna asserts the moral right
to be identified as the author of this work.

Printed in India by
Replika Press Pvt Ltd
310-311 EPIP Kundli
Haryana 131028 India

To Satyajit and Nooreen,
for whom I began to tell stories

Light breaks where no sun shines;
Where no sea runs, the waters of the heart
Push in their tides

—Dylan Thomas

Contents

Winter Evenings

Dr Anand unlocked the door and stepped into his house. The dark rooms were very cold. He switched on the light in the small living room. The window had been left open and the cold breeze had blown magazines and newspapers all over the room. Leaving his doctor's bag on the carved low table, he picked them up, folded them and put them back on the table. Then he went to the window to shut it.

Though it was only six in the evening, the cold, brittle darkness was crowded with stars. The Milky Way was a faint and distant smudge of white smoke overhead. The mountains were strong, dark silhouettes but he couldn't see the moon. It must be there, somewhere, he thought, for he could see the glistening sheen of the river in the wide valley. An icy wind rushed to his face, and with a sudden cold shudder he shut the window and drew the curtains.

Keeping his coat on, he went to the backyard to choose some firewood. Back in the living room, he set three neatly chopped pieces in the metal sheet drum known in those areas as the bukhari. Unfolding the newspapers, he pulled out the advertisement pages, crumpled these into balls and stuffed them under the wood. Then he opened the vent on top of the bukhari, poured in a few drops of kerosene oil, and dropped in a match. In just a few minutes the paper had given its fire to the wood. It sent the smoke rushing up the pipe that lead out through the chimney into the crystal night.

And from his window, higher up on the same hill, Rao saw the smoke rising. He was glad. Dr Anand was back and that meant that he could go over. The bank branch shut at two and the afternoons hung heavy on Rao. Sometimes he would go for a long walk to the monastery and back, to tire himself. But all of last week, the fierce afternoon wind had discouraged him. He had stayed in, reading disinterestedly and writing letters to people halfway across the world whom he hadn't seen in ten years.

So he felt good when the doctor was back. He tied a woollen scarf around his neck, folding the ends into his coat, raised his coat collar, pulled on his leather gloves and picked up a short, rounded stick. Ready, he stepped out into the cold.

It would be a long winter, and, inevitably, he looked up to the pass where the snow glistened in the night. Already the snow had been there for two months, cutting off the valley from the rest of the world. It would stay there at least another month, and then, if they were lucky, it would begin to melt.

The bank was crazy, sending him here. 'Baptism by blood,' he had been told! He had been a sucker to accept the offer. As if anybody cared what he did to disburse miserly loans to the handful of farmers here. It wouldn't make any difference. At least not in the winter and not if they couldn't keep that wretched pass open. His face flushed against the cold and his teeth set, he knocked on Dr Anand's door and quickly stepped inside.

'Come along, come along,' called out the doctor.

'Bloody cold.'

'Always cold, unless the sun is out.'

'When is the sun ever out?'

'Actually you are right, haven't seen it this week.'

Rao loosened his scarf and sat down, extending both hands towards the bukhari. He took out his pipe, and turning it around, tapped it vigorously on the palm of his hand. Dr Anand watched him do it but restrained himself from saying anything. He couldn't stand the sweet smell of tobacco that would hang in the room long after Rao left. He would have to open the window again at night.

Rao knew that the doctor would soon ask him what he would like to drink though he knew that the doctor only had whisky in the house, and that the doctor also knew that Rao preferred his whisky neat.

'What will you drink?'

'Whisky, neat, please.'

The doctor went to the little closet and took out the bottle of whisky. He had bought six glasses when he had gone down in the summer. Two had cracked during the journey but he still had four. 'Will never need more than two,' thought Dr Anand as he fixed the drinks. 'There's nobody in this village except Rao, blast him, that I can have a drink with.'

But when he turned back, he was smiling.

'Cheers.'

'Cheers.'

Rao took a small sip of his whisky and a few quick puffs from his pipe. Dr Anand pointedly moved his chair away before sitting down and then threw himself into it.

'What news?' asked Rao.

The doctor ran his fingers through his hair.

'A woman nearly died today.'

'What happened?'

'Allergy to anaesthesia. But she came out finally.'

'Good work.'

'Good luck, rather. How about you?'

'Dull day today.'

And usually, thought the doctor, your hole of a bank is a veritable hub of activity.

But aloud, he said: 'How come?'

'No mail, no work. Not one potential borrower.'

'They are all frozen, or sick. We really need that new hospital.'

Back to the new hospital, thought Rao, can't we ever talk of anything else?

And aloud: 'How's the work going?'

'The contractor says another four months, four months after the road opens, that is.'

'I'll be gone by then.'

'You'll get a good posting after this, you deserve it.' The doctor's smile was very pleasant, very friendly. But he was wondering what this city slicker had done to deserve anything.

Rao knew that the doctor would reach for the pack of cards secretly, mysteriously, as if he was going to come up with a great surprise, some marvellous Christmas present.

Dr Anand bent down and picked up the cards, hiding them in his cupped hands and then revealing them suddenly, in the manner of an oriental magician. Rao could have screamed.

'Rummy?' asked the doctor.

You don't know any other game, in any case, thought Rao.

'Okay, rummy.'

Rao placed his pipe on the table. The smoke curled up gently to the doctor's nostrils and into his head.

Throw away that wretched pipe, he wanted to say.

The cards were dealt and the game began. The room had warmed up with the fire and a comfortable glow had spread gradually over the room. Each of them was alone with his glass, his ten cards and his thoughts.

A few weeks more of this, thought Rao. Then he would have better company in the evenings than a stuffy, small-town, self-centred doctor. He would be back in the thick of things, back in circulation. It was a pleasant thought. He took a large sip of the whisky. It seared his throat and he coughed.

My resident film star, thought Dr Anand. He must smoke a pipe and drink neat whisky even though he can't take it. Suffer him for a couple of months more and let's hope his replacement will be a more intelligent chap. Someone genuine and not an upstart.

Lost in thought, the doctor got up and put a small log in the bukhari. Then he blew at the dying flames and saw the blue licks rise again. He came back to the table and threw down a king of spades. Almost instantly, he realized that he had made a mistake. What a fool he was. He picked up the card quickly.

'Sorry, that was a mistake.'

Rao had seen this before. Tonight he would not let it pass. In his agitation he puffed at his pipe quickly and sent the smoke straight into the doctor's face.

'You can't pick it up, I say.'

'It's only a friendly game.'

'Friendly, my foot,' Rao was shouting now. 'It's cheating.'

'You call me a cheat, you…you pipe-smoking bank clerk.'

'I'm not a clerk. I'm the manager, you village doc, you vet!'

Dr Anand wouldn't be called a vet by anybody. With a short swift movement of his forearm, he slapped Rao across the face. Smarting from the blow, Rao slapped him back. Then he got up and walked out, leaving the door open to the chilly wind.

Dr Anand sat quietly for a long time. Then, slowly, he got up and put another log in the bukhari. When he washed the glasses and put them near the drinks closet, he was already hoping that he would need to use them the next evening.

Rao walked home and the chilly wind quickly blew away his anger. Perhaps he had been hasty to walk away like that. Perhaps he should go back and apologize, or at least he must do it tomorrow. He looked involuntarily at the snow on the pass. It looked so heavy, so permanent.

Raya

My secretary brought in the message. I could see that he was trying to keep the excitement out of his voice.

'There was a call from Moscow, sir. A lady called Raya something...Raya Kanieva. She said she knows you.'

I searched my memory for that name. My stay in Moscow, a short stay of a year and few months, was more than a quarter-century old. I drew a blank.

'I don't know anyone by that name.'

'She left her number. May I connect you?'

'I don't know her.'

'She is some very desperate lady, sir. She says she is dying.'

I looked up from my papers. Something told me that my day would not move ahead unless I put this behind me.

'Okay, let's see what this is all about.'

'I'll connect you from here itself, sir.' He was carrying her number on a yellow slip and clearly did not want to miss listening in on this conversation.

When I took the line, the voice at the other end was even, clear, unhesitant and the English that the lady spoke was very good, unaccented.

'Thank you for speaking to me. Your name is N.?'

'Yes, that's right.'

'The Indian Embassy in Moscow gave me your number when I told them that I was looking for a writer by this name. You are a writer, no?'

'In a way, yes. How can I help you?'

'You met me. Don't you remember? A long time ago.'

'I'm sorry, I don't recall... In Moscow?'

'Yes in Moscow... Remember, when you had come here. In 1953?'

'1953? Madam, there is some mistake... I wasn't even born in 1953.'

I saw my secretary's eyes widen. Clearly, this was living up to his expectations.

'You were not even born?' the voice seemed to trail off, as if she was running out of hope.

Then she spoke again, in a rush. 'It was 1953. I was only sixteen. You were here for the Conference of Writers. I remember everything... Now I am over seventy. The doctors tell me that I have only a few weeks to live. I...I am dying.'

Something in her voice, perhaps the clarity of her memories, or the underlying desperation, made me think. This was not some crank call. This Raya Kanieva, whoever she was, knew what she was talking about. When I spoke again, I was already on her side. 'I think, madam, you are mistaking me for someone else that you met. It is true that my name is N., that I am a writer in my spare time, that I was also in Moscow for a short while. But it is also true that I was there in 1983, not 1953.'

There was a long silence. She was trying to grapple with what I had said.

'But sir, the person I met in 1953 was also a writer...and the same first name. We became friends. And then he left for India. There were a few letters but nothing after some time, nothing now for more than fifty years. I, too, had stopped looking for him. But now I am dying...only I know what he has meant to me all these years.'

Fifty years and more, I thought. Perhaps there was a writer by the same first name who had met a young girl in Moscow. But then, perhaps he was already dead. The thought seemed to reach her.

'I know, it's been a long time. Please sir, can you help me find him?'

'I'll try,' I said. A faint recollection of someone of the same name that I had read about was already forming at the edge of my mind. 'But I cannot promise anything.'

'Only promise me that whatever news you have—good or bad— you will tell me. Only please don't give me silence.'

'I will tell you whatever I can find out,' I promised, and put down the receiver. Then I thought it only fair to relate to my secretary the part of the conversation that he had not heard.

'Love story, sir, love story,' he said. Then he looked up sharply. 'Maybe someone from your past life, sir?'

'Nonsense,' I said and closed the conversation.

I tried to put the incident out of my mind. After all, I told myself, what could I possibly do? But the unhesitating voice, the clear diction of Raya Kanieva kept drumming insistently in my head...*I am dying...please help me...only don't give me silence*...the plea, plaintive at first, began to grow in my mind until it seemed that she was shouting at me from every side. Finally one afternoon, I pushed away my papers, got up from my desk and opened the windows. The hot summer wind that blew in seemed to quieten the voice in my head, at least for a while.

But I knew then that there was no getting away from it. No amount of hot summer wind would free me of Raya's dying plea... Mine is not a very common first name and all of us anyway come from Punjab. So a few well-placed queries is all it took. Yes, there had been a writer with the same first name. He had been a Punjabi writer, known mostly in Punjab for a literary magazine that he had started and edited for several years. The magazine still came out but not too regularly. Perhaps the man was no more, I thought, or had run into money trouble, or perhaps this was simply the way of all literary magazines. There seemed only one way to find out.

If one takes the Shatabdi Express from New Delhi to Kalka, as I did that Saturday morning, it's possible to reach Pinjore in about six hours. Most of the passengers on the Shatabdi get off at Chandigarh, and when the train pulls into Kalka it mostly carries the tourists bound for Shimla. I left them as they rushed towards the toy train for the last haul up the mountain and walked towards the cycle rickshaw stand.

The Kalka bazaar lay deserted in the afternoon heat. The shops were open but most of the shopkeepers were sleeping under the ceiling fans knowing that nobody would bother to come out shopping till the sun's fury abated. Then they would all come out to buy vegetables, or to go to the mandir at the northern end of the bazaar, or simply to eat kulfi with faluda at Ishar Sweets. But there was virtually no one around at twelve-thirty in the afternoon, not even at Ishar Sweets, and my cycle rickshaw went swiftly down the slope of the bazaar, until it reached the railway crossing from where I could see the hills shimmering in the afternoon haze. Then quickly we were in the narrow, twisting Pinjore bazaar. When I could see the walls of the old Mughal garden, I knew that I was somewhere near my destination but the rickshaw-wallah could not help me further. We stopped at the last shop in the bazaar, a dhaba with its rows of gleaming brass pots and pyramids of bright red tomatoes. The bald dhaba owner, his florid face and pate reflecting the fire from his tandoor, did not even look up from the potatoes that he was chopping with practised precision.

'Take the next lane on your right and go till the end. It's the second house after the old baoli.'

The baoli still had some water in it but it was not clean. Centuries ago, at the time the Mughal garden was laid out, it must have supplied drinking water to all of Pinjore village. Now there was moss on the wide steps that led down to the black water. Old, small houses with little verandas huddled close to each other. I found the house I was looking for. The rolled-up bamboo chicks had been let down to shelter the veranda from the afternoon sun. A street dog slept near the three steps that led up to a door painted chocolate brown. He opened one eye briefly as I stepped around him and then went back to sleep. The brass bell had an old fashioned ring that seemed to reverberate back into my hand.

When the door opened, I did not need to introduce myself. The lady, the old writer's wife, was waiting for me.

'Please come inside. It's very hot today. You must be very tired. Let me put on the fan.'

Hurriedly she welcomed me into the shaded room and switched on the fan. Then she quickly went into the house and in a few minutes was back with a tall glass of sweet cold nimboopani. I thanked her and as my eyes adjusted to the relative dark, I could see that she was in her sixties. But her hair was barely touched by grey, her step and voice were firm, and her light green salwar kameez made her look much younger.

'Lunch will be ready in a few minutes,' she said, brushing aside my remark that I had actually eaten something on the train.

'I know what is served on these trains—breakfast fit for a sparrow.'

As she went in again, this time to look at the lunch, I found myself looking straight at a black-and-white photograph of the writer whose name I shared. I walked up to it and looked into the large sensitive eyes and then stepped back to take in the neatly tied turban, the carefully folded beard, the full sensual lips, the jacket with the closed round collar. It was clearly a portrait taken in a studio.

'That was taken when he was twenty-eight.' I hadn't realized that the lady was standing at my shoulder. 'That was the portrait they used on the jacket of his first novel.'

'When was that?'

'It would have been '53-54. We were not married; we were married in 1955... But please have some lunch first.'

1953. I wished I could, for a moment, take that portrait far away to a dying woman in a snowbound land and show it to her and ask, is this the man you are looking for?

The lunch was simple, but hot and fresh. Parathas stuffed with methi with blobs of white home-made butter, fresh beans, mango pickle and a glass of thick lassi.

'It's nice,' she was saying, 'that you have the same first name as my husband. It is not a very common name; it makes me feel that you are one of our own. That is why I did not make anything special.'

As we ate at the small dining table, I noticed that there were books everywhere, books in English, books in Punjabi. They were kept in neat rows, in bookshelves, along the window sill, and in neat piles, on a table, even on top of the refrigerator. And they were obviously cared for; it seemed to me that each book was dusted every morning and then put back into its place. I wished then that I had not, in my big city way, made this a three-hour mission, all to be finished before I took the evening Shatabdi Express back to Delhi. I wished I had kept enough time to look at each and every book in this carefully ordered, shaded room.

She seemed to read my thoughts.

'Please eat peacefully. Then we will have tea and talk of everything you want to. There is enough time before the evening train.'

I spoke only after the tea had been brought in, in flowery mugs— tea that tasted of cardamom.

'Your husband wrote many books, worked so hard on the magazine. I haven't read all that he wrote, only some things.'

'You are searching for something in particular?'

'Yes, I wanted to know what he wrote about Russia. Did he go there?'

She looked up and met my gaze fully. She was silent for a few minutes, as if wondering how much to tell me.

'Yes,' she spoke carefully, half lost in thought. 'Yes, he did go there. In 1953. Just after his first book came out. We were not married then.'

'He wrote about it?'

'Yes, he was there only for a month or two. But it had a deep impact on him. He wrote a lot about his impressions, mostly political articles for the magazine. Also a long travelogue about a train journey. I'm sure I can find them for you but I don't know if you have the time today.'

'Yes, I wish I did...' I replied. After a moment's hesitation, though, I decided to tell her why I had come.

'Actually, it's not I but the person who asked me to look for him who doesn't have the time.'

The question hovered between us. I decided that I would tell her everything. I then told her about the strange phone call, about the coincidence of the name, of the desperation of someone who only had a few weeks to live. I did not know what I expected her reaction to be, certainly not what she did.

'I think I know what you are looking for,' was all she said as she got up and went into the other room. I heard a cupboard open and shut and then she was back. She was carrying a small blue and white suitcase, the kind that children at one time used to carry to school. She brought a dusting cloth and wiped the suitcase carefully on all sides, before she opened it. She then took out a thick black diary and leafed through it until she had found the page she wanted.

'This is written in English, unlike his other articles on Russia. I am not sure if he ever intended this to be read by anyone; in fact, he showed it to me many years after he had written it. But he is gone now and from what you tell me, I know he would not have minded my showing it to you?'

I began to read. Neat, well-formed, economical handwriting, in blue-black ink that so few people use nowadays, page after page…

When I reached Moscow, the last snow had already fallen—its remnants lay in small melting heaps. Even they would not last very long. It was the beginning of May and very soon the days would lengthen, the sun would become stronger, and warmer. The thin black ice on the roads and the wet cold would vanish. Everywhere there was the promise of beautiful days, long evenings, clear blue skies, young green leaves—just to look at those leaves took away some of the emptiness that I felt at being abroad, away from home for the first time, so far away that I could not bear to think of it. In its place there was a young hope, a slight head for adventure…a need perhaps, for love.

The first thing I noticed about Raya was how black her eyes were, how black her hair was. Just like the girls in India, I thought; and the way she spoke English, so clear, each word seemed to hang in the air just that instant longer, a frozen crystal. She had learnt her English at a special school, she said as we sat at a small round table in a simple café, and sipped light black tea with small pieces of lemon in it. I was surprised to learn that she too called it chai. 'Special school' meant that she was a child of some privilege but I did not ask any questions... I just wanted to hear her speak, and look into her black eyes. The first time I met Raya, I was almost ready to fall in love.

But I knew time was not on my side. I was only a visitor, and I would soon have to return... The days of walking around with Raya, listening to her, looking into her black eyes while sipping lemon chai would remain only a dream. Perhaps a dream wrapped up in a lace curtain with small flowers cut into it, the kind of curtain that covered the window of that twentieth-floor café. The café was hidden away in a hotel corridor, with its little round tables, the smell of strong coffee and piles of open sandwiches— cheese, salami and pickled cucumbers on black bread. The hostess, a woman with wide green eyes and a generous jaw, stood in front of rows of bottles of local brandy and vodka, and from the window we could see the large square—a square meant for parades, funeral processions, march pasts. Beyond lay the red walls of the Kremlin, the wide grey river in a curve, the domes of gold. In that café we used to meet and talk about books and poets. She had read all the classical Russian writers, and I had barely read a book or two of each. It took courage to show her what I wrote, I read it out to her, translated it for her into English. Her eyes glazed over as she listened, and once, a tear stole from her eye down her cheek. I reached out across the table and stopped it halfway with my fingertip...and there it froze, in its entirety... A slow smile caressed her lips, and it was I who looked away.

In the three weeks that I spent with her she wanted to tell me everything about her country, show me everything in that beautiful city—the churches with their onion domes, the museums, the metro and the new stations that were being built. I heard her and I did not hear her; I saw what she showed me and I did not. Because all of me seemed to be on a slow fire as I walked beside her on those wide streets, as I changed bus for train for tram...and at the end of the day all I would remember was how the weak sun softened the black of her eyes or how she gently stopped to pick up a leaf that had floated down from a branch to the pavement.

And when all the green—a bright spring green—leaves were on the branches, Raya turned me away from the city.

'You like Russia,' she said, 'but you cannot even know Russia until you have seen something of her countryside. Tomorrow we will go to the Silver Forest.'

She looked even younger than she was the next morning. She was dressed for a picnic. She wore a light blue shirt, and light blue trousers that ended well above her ankles, and even light blue canvas shoes. I felt out of place in my formal trousers and leather shoes, but I could not help it. I had gone to Russia to attend the Conference of Writers, and had not anticipated what was happening to me, not even at the fringes of my imagination.

'Don't worry. People will think you are a tourist, that's all. Just feel easy.'

For a long while we travelled in the metro, and then had to get off because the line was still under construction—it would be many years before the metro would go right up to the Silver Forest. So we got down and took a yellow bus and I watched the city thin down and open up to the vastness beyond. The suburbs had the feel and smell of new construction, the starkness of a new world where none had been, everywhere there were straight lines and right angles. I could feel Raya's eyes on me as I got my first glimpse of rural Russia, of little cottages with kitchen gardens, of small farms, of tall birches with scratched white trunks and fresh young leaves...

'It's different in each season,' Raya read my thoughts. 'In a few months it will all be red and then brown and then only white... When it is all covered in snow, you won't recognize it's the same place.'

When we reached the Silver Forest, it was as if I had walked into Turgenev's stories—a wide green bank led down to the curving Moscow river and on both sides was a birch forest; and over the trees across the bank rose the white face of a church with golden domes; and above it all was a faint blue sky, almost white.

'In winter you can see fishermen sitting on the frozen river, fishing through holes in the ice. But today we will take a boat.'

I managed to row the boat after some initial problems where I seemed to be taking the boat only in little circles. My arms and shoulders would ache for many days after that and blisters would form at the base of my fingers, but I wasn't thinking of all that then—I was listening to Raya recite poetry in Russian. I could not understand the words, but I could sense the rhythm and the passion. Over her shoulder I could see the summer sun glinting on the golden domes of the church in the forest and I knew that in such a setting the verses that she was reciting seemed the only thing worth writing, or listening to.

When I got tired of rowing we reached the bank and stayed there till the sun lost its fire and became weak and white, till there was no one else left in that entire Silver Forest except for her and me—two unlikely companions thrown together by some strange destiny, only to be separated by it again, but for the moment tied together by the love of verse and words. I, too, recited many poems to her that afternoon, everything I could remember, in fact. We didn't care what language they were written in—English, Urdu, Punjabi. There was no need to explain anything. Not as long as our fingers were entwined with each other... An artist's hands, she said, long fingers, maybe even a pianist's. Not meant for rowing boats. And then she laughed, and her jet-black eyes danced. She took my hands in both of hers and raised them to her lips.

I burnt with fever a few days after the visit to the forest, and the loneliness of being sick in a foreign land was with me. I could not go out to meet Raya as we had planned, and the next day she was at my door. I would never know how she had got past the icy blue eyes of the guards, who were stationed outside our hotel to keep the foreigners separated from the citizens. Perhaps there was something in the cut of her clothes or the confident jauntiness of her walk that had fooled the guard for a moment, and in that moment she had walked past, looking straight ahead.

She had never entered my room before, and when she did, it seemed as if the room had never been without her. Softly, gently, she walked barefoot around the room as she brought me cup after cup of chai with honey— her grandmother's recipe for all fevers. There was no need to even take medicines... I don't know if at night she left me alone to go home. All I do know is that when I woke up in the morning and opened my eyes, I found her black eyes looking at me. She smiled and went away, to make her *beloved chai with honey. This time, when she brought me the chai, I pulled her towards myself, but she resisted me for a moment.*

'I have been living in a monastery...' she said.

I don't think I understood her then as I gently pulled her closer. And when I looked up into the grey sky beyond the lace curtains I felt honoured and humbled to know that a human being could give so much, so generously. I yearned for time to stand still and wished that the fever would never end, that the day would stretch on forever, that the light that filtered through those lace curtains swaying gently behind that head of tousled black hair would be the last ever light of my life.

But the fever passed, and she left.

On the last evening we stood on the bridge and watched the river flow.

'Time to go home,' I foolishly said, and watched those black eyes fill with tears.

'Para damoi...' she responded in Russian. 'Yes, time to go home.'

I didn't know what to say to her. Her eyes told me that there was no need to say anything. Ours was the love of strangers, the meeting of two souls in a desert, which words could neither fathom, nor describe. Leaning on that bridge, we watched the evening turn into night, the lights come on in the huge hotel across the river, the water become black, the trees dark shadows. She slipped something into my hands. I looked at it closely in the dark. It was a book of Turgenev's stories, in English.

'You can write like him, I know.'

I held her face in my hands. Slowly I wiped the tears that were rolling helplessly down her cheeks.

'I will write,' I told her. 'And when I write I will always think of this night, this bridge, this river, this girl.'

I turned the page. There was nothing more to read, only a blank sheet of paper. It took me a long time to return to the room in Pinjore. I, too, had been in some faraway city, walking the bright summer streets, under the fresh green leaves, staring at the many hued onion domes of some church, against a bright blue sky. I, too, had lain quietly listening to a girl with faultless English diction, hearing her recite Russian verses, strum a moody guitar, watched her hand me glass after glass of weak tea, tea with honey...

'That's all,' the lady was saying as I broke out of my reverie. 'I think this is what you needed to see. No one has seen it before.'

I nodded. I had found my answers.

'And yes, one more thing,' she looked at me steadily. 'You can tell her it is safe.'

She reached up to the bookshelf and carefully pulled out a slim book. It was a volume of Turgenev's stories in hardcover, the author's portrait on its paper jacket, fading but intact. I held the book for a moment—*First Love* was its title—and then handed it back to her. Wiping it with her dupatta, she put it, gently, back in its place on the shelf.

In a few minutes it was time for me to leave for the railway station. As I began my walk I looked up thankfully toward the lilac hills. Raya could die in peace; I was not going back with silence.

Madam Kitty

The day Madam Kitty walked into the house, I looked up to the clear blue sky and thanked, with all my heart, the divine power that had sent her to us.

It had been twenty-five days, that day, since Mother came back from the hospital, and each one had passed with its daily arguments and conflict. Despite the blackout that took her to the hospital, now that she was back, Mother wanted to run the house as she always had. For forty years it had run to a tight, unfaltering schedule, as she endured the lonely years without my father, teaching at school and bringing me up. Even when she slept, for five short hours with the blanket drawn up over her eyes, she did not let go of the threads that held the house together. She knew how much milk there was in the fridge, which towel needed changing and which plant needed to be watered twice every day—just after sunrise and just before sunset. She would wake up in the dark, relentlessly, day after day, and put the house on its feet before she left for school. Immersed in the heady sleep of youth, I resented those early morning sounds, the sputtering of taps, the clang of utensils, the squelching of rubber slippers on a wet bathroom floor. The two servants stood by helplessly, young bleary-eyed boys with glasses of milky tea in their hands, tasselled woollen mufflers twisted around their necks, their feet bare on the cold marble floor of the kitchen. They waited for Mother's instructions and helped only when she asked them to. Only the most elementary tasks were left to them, where they could make few mistakes. They could sweep the floor but Mother had to remind them, each morning, that they should roll up the carpets and sweep under them; that they should not skip the part behind the big sofa; and that they should pull out the empty suitcases before sweeping under the double bed. They could go and stand in a queue in front of the milk booth and get the bottles when the white milk van lumbered up, or they could fill water in the water coolers, or they could tie up the bamboo blinds in the summer (exactly as she had taught them). They could put the water to boil for the tea, but *she* would add the tea leaves, in the right instinctive mixture of red and green label. She would not let go, even when her head throbbed with high blood pressure in the mornings and her knees were swollen with arthritis. Not until that morning, when she collapsed on the carpet and had to be rushed to the hospital.

With the exception of the time I was born, Mother had never visited a hospital beyond its outpatients' department. She did not trust hospitals just as she did not trust servants. She had always preferred to treat herself, managing her high blood pressure and arthritis like leftovers from dinner. To be covered up with old plates and stacked in appropriate corners of the fridge—things which should not be forgotten but not allowed to come in the way. She feared that hospitals would take this management out of her hands, like an ambitious servant might try to take over her kitchen, and she would never be in control again.

But once she was in the hospital, on a white metal bed with large white pillows, with an oxygen mask on her face, she gave in with a relish. She just lay back, her thin arms flat along her sides, her hair fanned out on the soft pillow, and let the doctors and nurses do as they wished. I watched from the visitor's chair, my surprise hidden behind a newspaper, as she took handfuls of coloured pills from the nurse and swallowed them quietly. Three times a day, without wanting to know what they were or why she was taking them at all. And resting against the raised pillows she ate whatever they brought on a white plastic plate, not caring what the vegetables were or how finely they had been chopped or whether they had been washed properly. Once, just once, she asked for an extra orange.

One evening as I watched her combing her steel grey hair contentedly, I said, 'If you had always been so relaxed, you wouldn't have fallen sick.'

'I can't help it,' she replied. 'I am what I am.'

For those fifteen days, she was a model patient for the doctors. For me she was a stranger. I wondered whether the hospital would change her forever.

Nothing, however, appeared to have changed the day she came home, her fifteen days with the doctors neatly typed, classified and spiral-bound in a plastic folder. The folder was put on a shelf with other important papers—rent statements, bank passbooks, certificates of recognition from the school. It became another object which had to be aligned and dusted every morning, and which the servants could not be trusted to handle properly. Once the folder had been put into its proper place, Mother began systematically to flout all the advice about regular medicines, minimum physical exertion and careful dietary habits that had been written into it. All she wanted to do was to take control of the neglected house once again. And of my life, if I gave her half a chance.

'That's all for doctors and hospitals,' she said petulantly when I asked her to follow the medical advice. 'I know my own system better than any doctor born yesterday. At my age I know when to take my medicines and when to sleep and when to eat.'

'Of course you don't. Otherwise you would not have fallen sick,' I tried to bully her. 'If you don't rest and do all that the doctors said you must, you'll go back to the hospital.'

'Don't talk to me like that. You may be forty years old for the rest of the world but don't forget who diagnosed your chicken pox when that fool of a doctor said it was allergy to soap.'

I knew there was no arguing with her when she was like that. She was, as she said, what she was. But she had listened to doctors and nurses in the hospital. She might listen to a nurse at home. That was when, in response to my imaginatively worded, furtively placed advertisement, Madam Kitty walked up to our doorstep.

She wore a very strong perfume. It entered the house in front of her like a shield. And when she sat down, comfortable and confident, in the armchair, it spread itself thinly through the room.

'I am a trained nurse,' she said in a direct, straightforward manner. 'I am forty-nine years old and would be very grateful if you appointed me.'

I guessed she was native to the city, but couldn't be sure. At first sight, she looked older than forty-nine to me. Perhaps it was vanity that had made her keep her age this side of fifty, while still choosing a figure high enough to be credible. Or perhaps a tough life had made her age quickly. Or perhaps, I thought, it was only the clothes she was wearing: a flowery blouse, which had the soft shine of cotton that has been washed and ironed too often, and a long brown skirt which showed signs of repair in one or two places. She wore high-heeled shoes that would have been in fashion many years ago but were clearly run-down now and out of shape. The only part of her outfit that was fresh and bright was her thickly laid red lipstick. It was obvious that she needed the money.

It will remain a mystery to me what Mother liked about Madam Kitty, but she took to her instantly and completely, as if she had been waiting for her all her life. She did not complain about her perfume or her red lipstick, and submitted to her efficient discipline like she had submitted to the doctors and nurses at the hospital. I marvelled at the transformation; this was not the mother I had lived with all the forty years of my life. But I was not complaining. I was once again able to go about my life guiltlessly, certain that Madam Kitty had taken care of everything to Mother's full satisfaction. She would be there in the morning, in time for Mother's breakfast. She would help her with her toilet and her clothes and supervise the cleaning of the house. Then, as I left for work, the two of them would settle down to mid-morning coffee and conversation. On the rare Sunday when I was at home, I watched in admiration how Madam Kitty ensured the servants bought the right vegetables and meats, fresh from the market, and had lunch ready on time. After lunch she would doze off on the armchair while Mother took her nap. Sometimes, if it was not too late, I would see her in the evenings, fussing around Mother, counting out her medicines for the night's dose.

For three months Madam Kitty ran our house to perfection, just as Mother would have wanted it—and, to be honest, just as I would have wanted it as well. I had grown used to Mother's way of doing things and I was uncomfortable if I ever had to spend a night in another house or a hotel.

One evening, after Mother had gone to bed, Madam Kitty came into the drawing room where I was working on a magazine feature I had to submit the following morning. She stood next to the sofa, and when I looked up to wish her goodnight before she left, I saw her watching me closely with her intense black eyes. She smiled, looking much younger than forty-nine.

'Don't work yourself so hard,' she said. 'You look very tired.'

As she spoke, she reached out and patted my shoulder in light-hearted concern. Then she put her white leather handbag on the centre table and went past me into the kitchen. She returned a short while later with a cup of tea.

'You need this. Why don't you get married so you have a woman who can make you a hot cup of tea when you come back in the evenings? It can make all the difference and it's not too late, believe me. I'm sure your mother will like that, too.'

She watched me as I had the tea, a gentle, indulgent smile playing around the corners of her lips. Then she glanced into the antique mirror that hung on the wall above my shoulder and exclaimed:

'Oh my God! I am a mess.'

She pulled out a long black comb from her handbag and ran it smoothly in quick motions through her hair. I watched as she patted the brown-black hair almost unconsciously towards the centre of her head where it had begun to thin. Then she took out a lipstick from the bag, twisted it open and applied a thick, wet coat of red to her lips.

'Now that's much better, isn't it?' she said. 'At my age a woman has to take extra care of herself. It's so easy to let go.'

Then Madam Kitty gathered up the tea tray and put it away in the kitchen. As she stepped out of the house, she turned and gave me a little quick wave which seemed as much a promise as a farewell. Confused, I fought a lonely, losing battle with her strong perfume that had spread its tentacles all over the house. In the end, I consoled myself with the thought that she was a good and efficient nurse and that my mother was happy with her.

Some days later, when Madam Kitty was filing her nails and having tea with me, reclining in the drawing room armchair, I opened the door to find Dev standing outside. I hadn't seen Dev for months but that did not bother me. He had always made a point of not being in regular contact, not committing himself to any constant relationship. He would turn up for a few days, then vanish again, and turn up again some weeks or months later. He did not like to be asked any questions and I did not mind. I noticed that he had grown a slight, grey beard. But for that he was the same—blue jeans, white cotton shirt open at the neck, brown moccasins, thin red lines in his eyes, which people often wrongly ascribed to too much drinking.

'Hello, old friend, remember me?'

'Come in,' I said. 'I suppose I shouldn't ask where you've been.'

'I've been places,' he said, stepping inside and hugging me strongly. 'Give me dinner and I'll tell you all about it.'

I introduced him to Madam Kitty. They nodded to each other. Madam Kitty finished her tea quickly, and picking up her bag took her leave. I saw her off to the door and came back to Dev.

'Let me get you something to drink and then you can tell me about all your adventures.'

Dev followed me to the kitchen and helped with taking out the ice from the fridge as I poured the drinks.

'This lady,' he said, concentrating on releasing an ice cube out of the plastic tray, 'this lady who was here—who is she?'

'Madam Kitty? She's the nurse I've had to keep for Mother.' Then I told him about Mother's illness, the days at the hospital, and how difficult it had been to handle Mother on my own.

'She's quite efficient,' I concluded. 'Mother's like an obedient child in her presence.'

Dev was silent for a while and we went back to the drawing room. He took a sip of his drink and lit a cigarette. Finally, he spoke:

'Well, she must be a good nurse if you say so. But you can take my word for it, she certainly was a good whore.'

'What?'

'Yes, she was a regular on Marine Drive in the evenings. Three or four years ago.'

'Are you sure?'

He looked at me and smiled.

'I don't forget my women, especially those with whom I've been more than once.'

Then, for some reason, both of us burst into laughter at the same time. We laughed loudly and boisterously, like schoolboys sharing a lewd joke. We quieted down only when Mother came into the room wondering what had happened.

From the next day, everything about Madam Kitty began to irritate me—her cheap, strong street perfume, her garish red lipstick, her little coquettish waves and smiles. I tried to stay out of the house if I knew she was there. And if she still happened to be there in the evenings, I would not sit down to have tea but stand around impatiently, waiting for her to leave. Her efforts at kindness, her tender ways with my Mother, her efficiency and hard work only infuriated me now. I struggled for a way to tell Mother that her good nurse was only an ageing out-of-work whore.

One night, sitting down at my desk to write an important personal letter, I could not find the pen with which I always wrote such letters. It was an old, dark red Parker 51 with a silver cap. I searched through the drawers of the desk but could not find it. Madam Kitty must have stolen it, I concluded. There was no one else who had access to the house. A whore and a thief! A person with no character would not think twice before stealing a pen; tomorrow it could be anything else. Immediately, I told Mother that Madam

Kitty had quick fingers and had taken my pen. She had to go; we couldn't let a thief walk around the house all day.

The next morning, I told Madam Kitty that we would not required her services any longer. Mother was much better and felt that she did not need help all the time. She wanted to feel independent and in control again. Madam Kitty listened to me calmly, as if she had been expecting this to happen. I had already calculated the money due to her, and handed it to her in an envelope. Quietly, she folded the envelope in two and slipped it into her white purse.

Then, looking directly at me, she spoke for the first time that morning.

'Why are you doing this?' she asked. 'I've been a good nurse to your mother, and you know she still needs me.'

I hesitated, fumbling for an answer. But she had already turned away and was heading for the door.

I did not tell Mother that I found the pen stuck in a book the same day. Even now, sometimes when I write with it, Madam Kitty's intense black eyes haunt me. They seem to say that, after all, she was doing a good job.

The Superintendent's Formula

The evening fell quickly in Jalgaon, especially in winter. It rushed over the tiny town as if it had been hiding at the outskirts, waiting for a signal. Oblivious to the gathering gloom outside, Biswas carefully locked up the two-roomed customs check post. It was a very ordinary office without any really important papers or cash receipts. Nevertheless, Biswas was a man of regular habit. He first cleared his wooden desk with the dark green top, and wiped it with a folded duster. He put away the ink pot and the set of red and blue desk pens into the drawer. Then he tied up the few files he had been working on in their cloth-backed flaps, and stacked them neatly in the steel cupboard. He took a look around and straightened the registers on the shelf so that they lay edge to edge. He shut the solid, wooden flaps of the barred little window and then turned with folded hands towards the picture of the Goddess that hung near the door. He always prayed in the evening before leaving office. Then he switched off the light and shut the door, turning the key in the heavy brass lock. Switching on the naked bulb in the tiny veranda, he stood for a moment in thought.

As far as he could tell, all the papers were in order for the Superintendent's visit the next day. Not that the Superintendent would want to see too many papers. He came from his office, seventy kilometres away in Haripurduar, for a very specific purpose—to assess the customs duty to be paid on their baggage by officers at the end of their tenures in the neighbouring country where they worked on various development projects. The Superintendent was the only officer in the entire region who had the powers to assess duty. He was a very important man for these officers, who would be returning with their precious refrigerators, colour television sets and video recorders. He could clear their baggage at the cheapest rate if he wanted. So, a week or two before their baggage actually came down from the hills, they would send him a telegram and set up an appointment with him either in Jalgaon or, more often, in the much more pleasant town of Tajoding, which lay across the border, face to face with Jalgaon.

Biswas had no power to assess customs duty. He was only an inspector. His job was to prepare the forms, in which the Superintendent would fill in the magic figure, and the permits that the Superintendent would sign in triplicate. And then, when the baggage actually came down, he would let it cross the border check post by lifting the barrier. The barrier was nothing more than a long log painted white and weighed down at one end by a huge triangular stone. Of course, as an inspector he always had the right to conduct a spot check on the baggage to make sure that what was going through tallied with what had been declared. In the eight months that he had spent on the Jalgaon check post, he had never summoned up the guts to refuse to lift that barrier. That is not to say that he hadn't been tempted to experience at least once the full power his job entitled him to. But innate caution had told him that the Superintendent, having made a special visit to sort out things with the departing officer, would not appreciate a spot check. Perhaps if he had, just once, done a spot check, it would have increased his importance. Then they would all have treated him with proper respect. Now they were polite to him, just enough to make sure that he didn't become a nuisance. As things stood, it was the Superintendent who really mattered. It was he, and not Biswas, who would be taken out to Tajoding for a good lunch. Tomorrow would be no different, thought Biswas, as he walked to his little quarter that lay a hundred yards from the check post. Mr Saxena, who had been working on a hydroelectric project in the hills for the last five years, was being transferred back home. Like the others, he would turn up, fawn over the Superintendent, and take him away for the better part of the day.

Biswas unlocked the door of his quarter and walked in. The two small rooms were bare. There was a small table, and a string cot with a thin pillow under a dark green, checked bed sheet. There were two metal trunks, covered with a red sheet. A cushion with an embroidered cover and mirror work was the only sign of comfort. A naked bulb hung in the centre of this room.

The second room had a wooden cupboard that had been written off in the records of the office and moved to his quarter. A small rectangular mirror had been nailed in on its side, and next to the cupboard, in the narrow window sill lay a shaving brush, a razor and a few bottles. The other half of the room served as a kitchen. An oil stove and a few utensils lay in the corner. It was just enough for him, Biswas often thought. After all, what else did he really need? His wife and two and a half-year-old son were in the village. It wasn't too far, but there hadn't seemed much point in bringing them with him. This way he could save a few extra rupees and take some things for them whenever he went back to the village. He could never say when he would be moved to another place. These border check posts were in high demand.

A persistent knocking on the door woke him up earlier than usual the next morning. He could hear a vaguely familiar voice.

'Telegram for you, Biswas babu.'

The word 'telegram' made Biswas get up from his cot quickly. He knotted his thin cotton lungi around his waist and rubbing his bare chest with the palm of his hand he unlocked and opened the door. It was Kanhaiya from the post office. At that hour he was not in his khaki uniform, but had walked across in his pyjama and a white vest with an angular pocket stitched across the chest. He had a toothbrush in the corner of his mouth.

'Wake up, wake up Biswas babu. Or the world will pass you by and you can live on in your colourful dreams. Telegram for you.'

Shifting his toothbrush to the other side of his mouth he pulled out a folded pink telegram from his angular pocket and handed it over to Biswas.

Biswas rubbed a hand over his face. He had not even had the time to look at the calendar with the painting of the Goddess. It was not auspicious to look at people like Kanhaiya early in the morning. God alone knew what kind of a day would follow. He took the telegram with an unsteady hand. He could not remember when he had last received one, and his mind raced back to his wife and son. There had been a bad epidemic of cholera in some of the villages. With a jerk, he tore the edge of the telegram. Kanhaiya was still waiting in the little veranda, chewing on the toothbrush as he watched Biswas's face intently.

'I hope all is well, Biswas babu?'

'Yes, yes, all is well, all is well.'

But Kanhaiya still stood there, leaning against the wooden pillar which held up the corrugated cement sheet of the roof, his nonchalant attitude scarcely disguising an intense curiosity.

'It's official,' Biswas's tone had changed. 'It's from the Superintendent—he is not coming.'

'Well,' said Kanhaiya, 'that's your business and his. I'll be on my way. I have to get ready and start distributing the letters. Diwali is coming next week and there is a sack full of greeting cards.'

With a deep gurgling sound, Kanhaiya spat out the toothpaste in a little, tight wad straight into a muddy puddle and, holding up his pyjama with his left hand, walked off towards the road.

Biswas watched him go in the dewy, faint light of the early morning. Then he went back into his room, bolted the door and reread the telegram. As he had told Kanhaiya, the Superintendent was not coming that day. He had not given any reasons. What he had not told Kanhaiya was that the Superintendent had also instructed him to attend to the case of Mr Saxena, which had already been scheduled, and had given him the authority to assess duty on the baggage all on his own. Carefully, Biswas folded the telegram and put it on the window sill next to his shaving brush. He had better get ready. It was going to be an important day.

By nine, after a bath and shave, he was in the office. He had worn his terry cot uniform shirt, and his belt and shoes shone with fresh polish. As soon as the peon came in, Biswas gave him quick instructions.

'Hurry up Devji, clean the office, open the windows. We will be receiving a visitor at ten-thirty, a very senior officer. Please give him tea in the teacups, not in your usual glasses. The cups are in the cupboard and please bring them in the tray. And keep the water on the boil so that you can bring in the tea quickly.'

Devji squinted at Biswas through his thick spectacles in surprise. Biswas had never asked for tea in the teacups, not even when the Superintendent came. He always said that he preferred tea in the ribbed glasses; it stayed warmer that way. Then shrugging his shoulders, Devji climbed on the office stool, took out the cups from the top shelf of the cupboard and went out to wash them.

Mr Saxena did not come at ten-thirty and not even at eleven. Biswas watched the road anxiously through the barred window. Finally, a blue and white four-wheel-drive jeep drove up to the check post and stopped. Biswas recognized the vehicle of the hydroelectric project. This would be Mr Saxena.

'Please come in, sir, please come in and sit down,' Biswas got up to greet Mr Saxena solicitously. 'Devji, tea please. In the cups.'

Mr Saxena was a short and heavy man and quickly sank into a chair after making sure that it wasn't too dusty. He took off his glasses and wiped them on the sleeve of his shirt.

'Where is the Superintendent?'

'He hasn't come today, sir.'

'Hasn't come? Why? The morning bus from Haripurduar has already come. I saw it standing in the market.'

'He will not be coming, sir. He has sent a message, a telegram, to inform us.'

Mr Saxena's anger and frustration was etched clearly all over his round face. If the Superintendent did not come, it would mean another trip down from the hills to clear his baggage. He did not have many days left before his move. When he spoke, there was agitation in his voice.

'But it was all fixed. He promised me over the telephone last week. That is why I have come down.'

'Don't worry, sir, your work will be done today. He has authorized me to be of full assistance to you. Please have some tea.'

Mr Saxena sank back into his chair in obvious relief. He smiled broadly at Devji who stood by his side holding the tea tray.

'Oh, why didn't you tell me that before, Inspector sahib. It's quite right also, of course, isn't it? You are here with how much, ten- or fifteen-years experience in this job, so why should the Superintendent travel all the way? It's such a waste of government funds when there is already a fully competent officer here to do the job.'

Mr Saxena talked all the while that he sipped his tea. He asked about Biswas's family, his health and his promotion prospects. Then he asked him about local politics in Jalgaon and about the state of the new road, which when completed would cut the journey to the nearest airport by half an hour. Biswas was overcome by the fact that Mr Saxena, such a senior officer, could pay so much attention to every word that he said in response. Usually when the Superintendent was there, he would barely glance at Biswas, make a polite remark or two, and then drive off with the Superintendent. But Mr Saxena had a lot of time that day. It was well after he had finished the tea that he leaned forward towards Biswas.

'Biswas babu, I haven't brought my papers here, you know. They are in the guest house. If you don't mind, perhaps we could go there and finish the work, and maybe have some lunch together?'

They climbed into Mr Saxena's vehicle and the driver honked and nudged his way through the trucks and cycle rickshaws and vegetable sellers until he reached the border post. Then he took a sharp right turn, and driving under an arched gateway crossed over into Tajoding. From there the road curved unremittingly upwards into the mountains. But quickly, they turned off the main road and passing by the playing field of a school, arrived at the guest house where Mr Saxena was staying. It was an elegant old bungalow with a small garden and an outhouse. A polite attendant opened the door and they sat down in comfortable armchairs in the pleasant veranda.

At a signal from Mr Saxena the attendant brought out two chilled bottles of beer from the fridge. After opening them, he rushed off to the kitchen in the outhouse and was soon back with a plateful of boiled eggs, cut in half and generously sprinkled with salt and pepper.

As the first glass of beer went down, Biswas felt a glow of well-being come over him. He relaxed back in the armchair and unbuttoned the collar of his uniform. The salted boiled eggs went well with the beer and he wondered why his generous host was hardly eating any. Probably some health reasons, he thought. Mr Saxena insisted on a second bottle of beer for Biswas, even though he had himself not finished the first. The attendant came and put the second bottle in front of Biswas.

'No, no, thank you. It will be too much. One has to do some work also, you know.'

'This is only water, Biswas babu. And lunch will take some time. Come, come.'

'Lunch? I have already eaten so many eggs.'

'We'll have a little something,' said Mr Saxena. He signalled again to the attendant and gave him two hundred-rupee notes. 'Nar Bahadur, run down quickly to the Royal and bring two plates of fried chicken and some hot tandoori rotis. And don't forget the pickled onions.'

While they waited, Biswas sipped his beer and watched the play of the sun on the veranda floor as it filtered through the green wire netting that had been fixed to keep the mosquitoes out. It was a pleasant feeling just to be out of the office.

Soon Nar Bahadur was back. He laid out the food on a low table between the two men. Biswas ate quietly and intently. It was good, rich food from an expensive hotel and he did not often get such a chance. The chicken bones piled up in his plate as Mr Saxena watched, smiling gently. It was only when the empty beer bottles and the plates had been cleared away that Mr Saxena reached for his briefcase.

'I'll show you all the papers, Biswas babu, and you can judge for yourself how much duty a salaried man like me should pay.'

Biswas began to go through the invoices.

'There are two television sets?'

'Yes, yes, I have bought one for my daughter actually. We have just fixed her marriage, you know.'

Biswas went through the rest of the papers. There was a refrigerator, a video recorder, a video camera and a music system.

'Of course, most of the things are used items,' Mr Saxena was saying, 'so you can easily depreciate their value, especially the music system. The children have used it so much. I should rather throw it away than pay duty for it. But you know, one keeps carrying half these things for sentimental reasons. You get attached to them.'

Biswas took a red ballpoint pen from his pocket and did some calculations on a small notepad. Mr Saxena took a pocket calculator from his briefcase and put it before Biswas in case he needed it. Biswas did the calculations on the notepad and then checked them on the calculator.

'Sir,' he said at last, 'you have to pay eleven thousand six hundred rupees as duty.'

'That is too much,' Mr Saxena remonstrated. And then, after a pause, he continued in a gentler, friendlier voice. 'Are you sure you have given me the maximum depreciation, especially on the music system?'

'Yes sir, I have not even included duty on the music system.'

'Please check again,' Mr Saxena pleaded. 'The Superintendent had told me that he would use a special formula by which I would not have to pay more than four thousand rupees. See that's the amount I have brought.'

Mr Saxena opened his briefcase again and took out four thousand rupees in two piles of notes, each secured by a thick rubber band.

Then he took out a folded envelope from the briefcase.

'And this is just for all your trouble, Biswas babu.'

'No, no, this is not necessary.'

'I know it is not necessary. But it'll make me happy. After all, you are a busy man and you have spent your entire day with me.'

Biswas's hand shook as he took the envelope and put it in the breast pocket of his uniform. Then, without looking at Mr Saxena he began to go through his calculations again. After a while he arrived at a figure, checked it on the calculator and looked up at Mr Saxena.

'For you, sir, using the Superintendent's formula, we can make the amount four thousand and fifty.'

Mr Saxena nodded keenly. He took out another fifty-rupee note from his wallet and added it to the four thousand rupees.

'I will have these deposited in the Jalgaon bank and my driver will bring you the receipts. I think the bank is open for another fifteen or twenty minutes.'

Biswas filled in the figure in the forms and signed the permits. Then he took out a stamp and stamp pad from his pocket and quickly put several stamps on the forms and the invoices. He handed all the papers over to Mr Saxena, who looked through them carefully and put them in his briefcase. He called his driver and asked him to drop Biswas back to the check post, and also to deposit the money in the government account in the bank. Then, smiling broadly, he warmly shook Biswas's hand.

'So it's all well done. And the Superintendent would have had to travel all the way just to do this! They should let you do the permits all the time. My baggage will be coming down next week. Of course, there is no need to check again, I hope.'

'Of course not, sir. There is nothing to check now.'

Back in the office, Biswas asked Devji to make him some tea. He took out the folded envelope from his breast pocket and opened it. There were five hundred rupees in it. Quickly he folded it and kept it back in his pocket. He made some entries regarding Mr Saxena's case in the registers. Then he carefully filed away the bank receipt that the driver had brought. He did not notice that Devji had brought the tea in a cup and not in his usual glass. For a while he sat, lost in thought, sipping his tea silently.

Soon it was time to close the office. He cleared away his desk and wiped it with the folded duster. Then he kept the ink pot away and placed the two desk pens into the drawer. He put the files in the cupboard and aligned the registers so that they lay edge to edge. He shut the window, switched off the light and shut the door. Then, in sudden panic, he opened the door again and switched on the light. He hurriedly made an apologetic obeisance before the picture of the Goddess that hung near the door. Then finally he went home, angry that, for a moment, he had nearly forgotten to pray.

A Death in Winter

It was on a yellow hot afternoon that we went to cremate my grandmother, with the kind of heat that makes you wish fervently under your breath for a death in winter. Nothing, not even grief, makes much sense in that kind of heat, when the roads give off whiffs of steam and the frame of the car window makes red scalding marks on your sweating forearm. A death in winter would be so much more sensible and decorous: the ice under the body would not melt away so fast into meaningless rivulets, the flowers would last a little longer, and it would be altogether more sad. It would give a proper chance to everybody, the aunts and the cousins, sisters and brothers, to grieve. Nobody could grieve in that burning yellow afternoon. Not properly, I mean.

Everyone was wilting by the time the black van pulled up at the gate. The driver got out, opened the back doors and waited, a doleful expression on his face. He had a rolled-up handkerchief under his grimy white, open collar. The sweat had drenched the handkerchief and now coursed into his vest. I remember with a strange clarity the way the drops glistened on the hair on his chest as I pushed past him, holding the body by the legs. Unlike what one would have thought, it had seemed all too simple, cold and mindless. Wrapping the white sheet around the body, putting it on the wooden stretcher and then tying up the middle and the feet. There had been no protests from that once all-powerful body, not even a single murmur of dissent. I remembered my aunt telling me once that the old lady's beauty and strength had been well known in the frontier town where she had spent her youth before the partition of the country. And once, when a towering, fierce

Pathan tongawallah had tried to abduct her, she had stood up in the tonga as it rushed downhill and fought with him until she had snatched away his whip and brought the tonga to a halt. There was no strength now in that dead heap which we pushed away in sad, tired silence. Hurriedly the driver shut the doors of the van and my aunts and cousins muffled their sobs.

There was not a whiff of wind that afternoon to stir the huge amaltas tree with its bright yellow flowers and dark brown rod-like pods, under whose shadow she had lived for twenty years. Everything was shrouded in a torpor of senseless heat.

As we stood around the pyre and helplessly watched the flames consume her I thought that her death actually belonged not to that summer but to the strange and blighted winter that had preceded it. She had in any case stopped living since that late October night, since that horrible shriek in the dark, and it would have been better if she had died then. Then, not only would we have been able to grieve properly, we would also have been able to dismiss her death as part of that cursed winter, in which so many had been written off. And we would have been able to remember her properly, like we had always seen her—ruddy, healthy, authoritative.

I was the eldest of sixteen grandchildren that she saw growing up, and I received the most of her love and indulgence. I liked the days when she would sit down on the double bed in the shaded bedroom in summer, or on the old sofas in the sunny winter veranda, and talk of the time when I was a little child. I loved to hear the story, and watch my envious cousins hear it, of the little tricycle my uncle had brought for me from Bombay and how I insisted on filling petrol in it in every corner of the room. And of the day when she had made the mistake of taking me to a butcher's shop, after which I was so miserable that I stopped eating meat till I was eleven. And it made me proud to hear that when she had taken me for long walks near the Safdarjang Hospital, which in those days was called American Hospital, there were no colonies beyond that point, only rock and gravel and thorny bushes and jackals.

I was the only one who had free access to her room, the citadel from which she ruled the family with a benevolent but firm hand. As I walked in and out of that room while my younger cousins watched from the door, it was impossible for me to believe that some day she would leave that citadel unguarded forever. Leave the hundred smells of that room—of dry fruits, of old perfume in round glass bottles with faded blue spherical dispensers stashed away in locked steel trunks, of expensive bath soaps—and simply go away, wrapped up unceremoniously in a sheet.

To me it had seemed that her reign over the citadel—and my unchallenged access to it—would last forever. Such was the strength in her voice and the colour in her cheeks and the determination in her walk. There was none of the other grandmother paraphernalia that I had seen in the houses of my friends. There were no sickbeds, no bedpans, no nurses coming to give painkilling injections every alternate evening on alternating arms, no cataract operations or green eye patches, not even a walking stick. Instead there was a relentless routine, as unbending as it was leisurely. There would be early morning prayers followed by a glass of milk with dry fruit. Then she would walk two kilometres to the gurudwara on the hill, which she had helped, in every way she could, to grow from a small wooden shed with a solitary gas lamp to an imposing gilded structure of marble and teak. She would be back for a light lunch cooked by one of her daughters-in-law and then she would sleep through the afternoon. In the evening she would go down the street with Mrs Khanna to the park with the four sections and a central fountain. After two rounds of the park they would sit on the bench near the fountain and talk until it was time for the evening prayers. And after dinner she always ate fruit—melon or mango or apple—and admonished any grandchild who dared complain that the fruits were not juicy or sweet or tasty enough.

I also had an idea, unlike my cousins, that she had not always been like this, so happy, healthy and commanding. I had heard, during my privileged presence in her room, whispered conversations of the dark days after the partition of the country. I knew something, too, about the photo album with the green and golden paisley binding which lay wrapped in a blue muslin cloth in the lowest drawer of the cupboard. In those black-and-white faded photographs taken by my father in the early fifties she looks very different, older than she did this winter, thirty years on. She has a hunted, fixed expression and her face with its deep-set eyes and sunken hollow cheeks is scary. She looks like a cardboard cut-out, a two-dimensional figure from whom the spirit has fled. She looks weak and sick, poor and hopeless. Once in a while, she showed me those photographs and quietly told me how they had survived the murderous frenzy of the birth pangs of freedom. Nobody dared to talk of those days openly in the family because my father had seen the killing and savagery so close that he would break out into a cold sweat if somebody mentioned a word. But I think she felt the eldest grandchild had a right to know, some right to keep alive memories, however gruesome, so that they were not all swallowed up irretrievably by the gathering years.

So sometimes, in whispers, she told me of those last weeks in Rawalpindi where the season of axes and swords and daggers had set in. She told me how they had hidden under beds from killing mobs, how they had moved from house to house escaping senseless death at every turn and how, finally, they had come out with only the clothes on their backs on one of the last chartered planes that flew out of Rawalpindi. She told me how she found, on arrival, that the same axes were out in Delhi and the streets on which she had expected joy and freedom and flowers had the same desolation, the killing, and the protesting, screaming, grotesque dead. She told me about the horror of waiting for my father and my grandfather, stuck in a locked-up office in Rawalpindi. And of fading hope as the days passed, until one day they knocked on the door and walked in, trembling. And only once did she tell me of her newly-wed daughter whom she had left behind and of whom there would never be another word, only one haunting photograph in that album. So I understood why the album, with its mysterious photographs, was always hidden away. It was a trick to sustain the miracle of survival.

The miracle was shattered that morning of the last day of October in 1984.

It should have been just another day in the normal, exciting beginning of a Delhi winter with all its promise of cold, bright joyousness. But that morning had ensured, in one dark moment, that there would be no thought that winter for love or play or for the flowers in the concrete traffic circles. An ugly cloud had loomed over the city that morning and a shadowy, cancerous anger was spreading through its lanes. By evening there was news of riots and killings on Ring Road, of cars being stopped and burnt, of houses being attacked, and the men pulled out and killed. And across the slow river, the fires were rising. The family sat and watched television, but the news came by the telephone which rang every few minutes. There was no knowing what would happen through the night as the fear and the frenzy increased.

My grandmother sat silently. She completed her evening prayers and said: 'Let us all go to Mrs Khanna's house. We'll be safe there.'

So the house was locked up and furtively the entire family moved into Mrs Khanna's house and huddled into the two back rooms. In the dark I stole up to the terrace and saw the fires light up the corners of the night, reminding me of the time when the magical strobe of the old Safdarjung aerodrome used to explore the dark night and guide the planes in. Delhi had once again dissolved into rock and thorn, haunted by jackals. When I rushed down and told my grandmother of the fires, I saw that the colour had gone out of her cheeks and she looked much older than I could ever remember. She put a tired hand on my shoulder, told me to go to sleep and turned to pray.

All night we waited for the mob and hoped it would not come. I do not recall if I slept at all. It must have been very late when we heard the shouting, the ghoulish laughter, the clapping and the unceasing wail from the horn of a car, stuck as it burnt. The mob was close to the house as we huddled in the darkness. I felt a cold hand around my heart and a fear, an indescribable mindless fear passed over me.

And then, as if from next door, I heard a horrible scream. It rose, hung in the night air and descended into a hundred piercing echoes. It tore the night into shreds; it went through my bones like a sword and left me trembling.

Then the mob had passed, leaving Mrs Khanna's house untouched. In the first light of early dawn I looked at my grandmother's face and saw the fixed hunted expression that I had seen only in those old photographs. Her eyes had sunk and her skin was ashen grey. She seemed to be in a trance and I thought she was praying. But she was only repeating mindlessly: 'They are coming, they are coming again. Hide the children. Everybody hide.'

That day she did not come out of that trance. Nor when she moved back to her house and into her room. Her routine fell apart. There was no daily walk to the gurudwara and even Mrs Khanna could not make her go to the park. She sat in her bed all day, looking endlessly at that single photograph of her lost daughter in the old album: 'They took you and they are coming again. This time you hide. All of you, hide.'

Then, five months later, when that cursed winter had turned into a yellow summer, she stopped breathing. It would have been much better if she had died in the winter, killed by that terrible scream.

It Was Drizzling in Paris

I did not recognize anybody as I stepped into the dining room of the Willingdon for a quick bite. Not that I really expected to know anybody. I had come to Bombay and the club after many years, hauled back to the city I had left two decades ago by a sudden business opportunity. The opportunity had fizzled out as soon as it had appeared and once again there was nothing to keep me here. But there was still time for the evening flight and so I went back for lunch to the club, afraid to explore a new place, which would only make me more conscious of the fact that I had been away for so long.

Nothing much had changed, neither the food nor the ambience. And by the time I called for the coffee, I had actually begun to feel comfortable for the first time in the last two days. The waiter, whom I signalled for the coffee, came and handed me a slip.

'The gentleman is in the lounge, sir. He said that you could have your coffee there.'

I looked at the slip. It contained a visiting card which simply said: Ravinder Kashyap, Advocate, Bombay High Court. I hadn't met Ravi in years. I had no idea that he was in Bombay or had become a lawyer. In fact the last time I had met him, I had stayed with him and his wife in Paris for a weekend, five or six years ago. I was faintly curious about him.

He was sitting alone in the lounge, and got up as soon as he saw me. 'Ravi,' I said, 'what a pleasant surprise.'

'Yes, I didn't want to disturb your lunch since I had already eaten, but I did want to meet you.'

'It's been a long time.'

'Yes, five years and three months.'

I was surprised that he remembered our last meeting so exactly, but I only returned his smile and sat down in the comfortable leather couch.

As I looked at him I tried to picture him as I had last seen him. He used to dress with a certain dash then, wearing his hair a little longer than most people and sporting a drooping moustache. Even his suits had been on the jazzier side and I had put it all to the effect of living in a city like Paris. Now, he had put on some weight. His hair was cut short and he had shaved off his drooping moustache. In his black formal coat and grey lawyer's trousers he seemed very much an establishment person.

He saw me watching him and smiled.

'Yes, I know what you are thinking. How I have changed, sobered down and all that?'

'Well, I was actually wondering how you ended up being a practising lawyer.'

'I always had a degree and perhaps I should have joined the profession all along, except I hated the thought of the courts and the small-time lawyers sitting on benches and the whole mess. But…'

He fell silent. I waited for him to continue but he began to pour the coffee instead. Then he took out a cigarette; he tapped it on the back of his hand in a gesture that, I suddenly recognized, was so typical of him. He put out the match with a vicious twist of the wrist and let it drop into the ashtray with a caressing gentleness. Leaning back into the sofa he took a deep drag on his cigarette and looked at me purposefully.

'You tell me how things have been with you since we last met. Let's not talk about me.'

When a man says that, it is clear that he wants to talk about himself but will instead go through the motions. I decided to play along. Briefly, I told him that I was still in the same line of business, still unmarried and that I still loved travelling and staying in hotel rooms. He listened with an intentness that my story did not deserve, until I fell silent. Then, with the same intentness, he looked into his coffee cup, as if he were looking at the dregs for signs of his future, or perhaps for keys to his past. I stole a quick look at my watch. There was at least another hour before I needed to leave for the airport and it seemed only fair to let him talk.

'I thought lawyers were fond of talking. But you seem to make only me talk—what about you? How's the family?'

He gave me a rueful smile. And then it seemed like I had opened a floodgate.

'Family? All that finished five years and three months ago, when you last met me.'

'What do you mean?'

'Didn't you notice anything strange at that time, I mean, in my wife's behaviour and all that?'

'Nothing at all,' I replied almost instinctively. I remembered Arti as a young, likeable and vivacious person with whom I had gotten along very well. She had seemed to care for Ravi. I recalled a twinge of jealousy I had felt when I saw her taking so much care to see that his suits were of the latest cut and shade and that his ties matched. For a couple of days she had even made me feel that perhaps marriage was not a bad thing after all.

'I thought it was only I who had missed out on everything. Didn't she say anything to you, you know, about...'

He was quiet for a minute or so and it was obvious that he was deciding how much to tell me, how deeply to involve me in the inner conflict that had now begun to show on his face. Suddenly he turned to me and his voice shook with emotion.

'Let me tell you, Shashi. Arti left me six months after that. And the man she left me for met her then, when you were staying with us.'

There isn't much you can say when a man tells you that his wife has left him for another man. I stayed silent hoping that he would do all the talking. But it was obvious that I wasn't only a chance acquaintance whom he had run into at the club and decided to talk to. In his mind, I was involved in the whole thing. I had been around at the time. Perhaps I could throw some light on the disaster that would help him understand what had happened. I then realized why he had remembered the time of our last meeting so precisely.

Having told me the worst at the outset, he now seemed unexpectedly calm and detached, and began to talk in a manner that gave one the impression he had told this story many times.

'You do remember that she used to be very fond of tennis?'

I recalled being taken aback by the almost obsessive way with which she had sat and watched the Wimbledon finals on television that summer.

'Yes, she did seem very interested and quite knowledgeable.' For some reason, my answer pleased him and he nodded.

'She was taking tennis lessons at that time in the afternoons, and this man was her tennis coach. A rather nice chap, actually. He even came home a couple of times for a drink. I would never have known, actually, so deeply did I love and trust her, if she hadn't decided to tell me herself. That's another reason why I still don't blame her at all for what happened. She came clean, she told me herself, rather than go on stealing on me.'

'I can't ever forget that evening,' he continued. 'She insisted that we go out and eat. We used to do that once a week, but she didn't want to go to any of our usual places. We walked around for a long while until we found a small café. I remember there was music playing in the background and they were showing a football game on a large screen. And there amidst all that noise and frenzy, she told me that she was having an affair with this coach.'

I looked at him. All of a sudden he seemed a very weak and sad man.

'You know what that can sound like? You wouldn't. You are not married. But after five years of marriage, it can sound like the end of the world.'

'What did you do?'

'I tried everything. I fought with her, accused her, tried to make her feel guilty and sorry. For days I tried to make up to her.'

'Make up to her?'

'Yes, in terms of time and attention. I took leave, I offered to take her for a European holiday. I dressed up more carefully and even began to exercise to get into shape.'

He smiled ruefully.

'You know those lines which preface *The Great Gatsby*:

> Then wear the gold hat, if that will move her,
> If you can bounce high, bounce for her too,
> Till she cry "Lover, gold-hatted, high-bouncing lover,
> I must have you!"

'But nothing worked,' he shook his head, 'it was far too late.'

'You mean...'

'No, she didn't just walk off. And that's why I can't really bring myself to blame her even now. She really tried. She said she didn't want to hurt me, that she cared for me. After all, you know, five years of marriage cannot just be wiped off at one stroke. A lot went into those five years. When I married her she was just a girl straight out of school. I taught her a lot.'

A note of pride had entered his voice.

'In the beginning she didn't even have the confidence to speak English, though of course she knew English having studied in a convent and all that. For three months after we got married, we didn't go out anywhere in the evenings. I would come back from office sharp at six. She would be ready with the tea tray, and we would spend the entire evening on our balcony. I taught her the kind of English that was being spoken in Bombay, including the slang. She was so keen that she picked it up all so fast. When we attended our first party after that, she was just fine. I was so proud of her. It didn't matter at all that she hadn't been to the university.

'And when we were transferred to Paris, it was like a dream come true for her. She wanted to learn French, she wanted to become an artist, she wanted to dance. It was as if she had come home. I did everything she wanted. Those first two years in Paris were just fantastic. She would be out all day, attending one class or the other, and in the evenings we would walk the city, meet friends; there was nothing wrong...'

With a sudden motion of his fist he hit the table hard.

'There was nothing wrong with her or me. Just that rotten fellow, that snake. He had no business to do this to her, or to me.

'After she told me all this, we tried for a while to recreate those years. I begged her not to leave me and she told me that she was sorry for all that had happened. For six months she did not see this man. She was good to me. But something had vanished and there was nothing we could do about it. It was strange. Both of us realized it at the same time. I wasn't surprised when she told me one night that she had met him again. I knew it had to be. This time there was no shouting, no recrimination. Just nothing at all. She just moved out. I even helped to settle her in, you know, her papers and things, and then I left. I just couldn't go on staying in the same city.'

I looked around and motioned to the waiter to get us some more coffee. There seemed no other way to get through the awkward silence that would inevitably follow. But Ravi hadn't quite finished.

'Tell me, Shashi, you know me. You even knew her in a way. Tell me, would you have acted differently?'

'I would have killed her. Or certainly thrown her out immediately.'

He shook his head slowly.

'Then you too blame her. Like so many others to whom I have recounted this. My problem is that I cannot blame her. She was, is, a good person, and I still love her.'

The coffee came and as I poured it I remembered with great clarity an afternoon in Paris with Arti. The way she had poured jasmine tea into little cups in a restaurant near the Louvre. It was drizzling and the old buildings had a sombre beauty under the grey overcast sky. We had spent three hours in the museum, and I had in fact enjoyed it. That was strange, because normally I am not one for museums. I tend to go through them the way one would walk through a cemetery and I would have, any day, preferred a drive into the country. But I had enjoyed walking through the halls of the Louvre with Arti. I had liked the way she laughed, all the way to her eyes. And the way she had insisted that after the tea, we should walk in the drizzle right down to the Eiffel and take the steps to the first level. We had stood and watched Paris below us, grey and beautiful in the rain, and silently, with our eyes, we had followed the timeless, lazy curves of the Seine. She had turned her face and given me a look that seemed to touch me where I lived. It was a look full of possibilities, full of life, youth and love. Yes, I remembered that afternoon very clearly.

But Ravi was speaking again. 'It was just, it was just...'

'Bad luck?' I added.

'Yes, bad luck and perhaps, perhaps I just lost her to Paris.'

And then he was silent and far away. I quickly drained the coffee and told him that I had to leave for the airport. We shook hands quietly and I hastily walked out of the club—hating all weak men and all weak women.

Delhi

In the beginning their fights were mostly about money. Or children. Both of them wanted money. Who didn't? Everybody they knew in Delhi wanted more money, Ajay thought, as he pulled the chair on to the little balcony of their two-bedroom flat and sat down, his legs stretched across to the wrought-iron railing. And the fights about the children were related to money. They couldn't have a child just yet. Vinita knew it too, and most of the time she agreed with him. Except when she was under the influence of her mother. He had learnt to expect that the day she visited the old lady in chiffon and pearls, about once a fortnight, she would come back all worked up. He thought bitterly that today as well her mother, eating sweet halwa with oversweet tea, must have given her the same old line about how Vinita was nearing thirty, and when she herself had been thirty, Vinita had been eight.

Damn her. Her days had been different.

She hadn't been working, for one. And definitely not as a model for saris. A tall, young, svelte model who had just made it to the cover of the city magazine and should right now be expecting some exciting, well-paid assignments. Anyhow, tomorrow, he was sure, Vinita would cool down and be her practical, sensible self again. Once she walked into the studio and the lights came on, she would again believe that having children would be an awful nightmare.

But tonight they had fought. An ugly, fierce fight. And just when he had been telling her to inform her mother that nobody could get anywhere in life these days if they were changing nappies half the night, Vinita had turned and gone to sleep. He envied her this sleep. He envied her the ability to just shut her eyes in the middle of an argument and escape. Through the open window he could see her sleeping peacefully, her bare arm flung across the pillow carelessly.

He couldn't remember when he had last slept like that. Nowadays he couldn't sleep unless he had at least one drink. Especially if he was worked up like tonight. Even on days when he wasn't tense or angry, he always felt very tired. Every evening he could feel the fatigue congealed around his eyes and a strange pressure at the back of his head pushing relentlessly outwards.

Slowly he began to unwind thanks to the bittersweet gin. As he relaxed, he discerned, beyond his anger and his fatigue, a faint promise in the summer night with its clean, empty street and an occasional laugh from a passer-by. The promise seemed to float in the air, redolent with jasmine, and it told him that, ultimately, things would be all right. One day, he would definitely make it.

The next day he took out Yogi's visiting card from the top drawer of his office desk. That's where he kept all cards that could someday be useful. All tied up securely with a rubber band. He must really get an electronic diary or at least a card diary with a proper indexing system, he thought. He looked thoughtfully at Yogi's card. He had last met Yogi about a year ago, at a tea party in the college lawns for ex-students. That's when Yogi had told him that though he had qualified to be a lawyer after college, he had preferred to join his father's firm of stockbrokers. On an impulse Ajay dialled the office number given on the visiting card and invited Yogi to lunch the next day.

Yogi was surprised and did not hide the fact. They both knew that they had never had much in common in college. Ajay had belonged to the elite hostel group of public-school boys who spoke better English and somehow always managed to look smarter even though they usually wore cotton shirts bought cheap from piles of export rejects and jeans deliberately torn at the knees. And Yogi had been a day scholar who could never belong to that group, no matter how hard he tried. Ajay remembered him, chiefly because even then he had a lot of money to spend in the cafeteria and because he came to the university in a car, his dark glasses mounted high on his head, with music blaring loudly from the cassette player.

But now over lunch, all these distinctions seemed far away and quite meaningless to Ajay. To him, now, Yogi suddenly seemed a very good contact and he wanted to kick himself for having neglected him so long. All contacts had to be assiduously cultivated, fattened, so to speak, for the right day.

Yogi was balding now. Not from the forehead like most people but from the back, strangely. To hide that bald patch at the back, he had grown his hair from the top of his head and it fell on his neck in a sort of ponytail.

'My father thought that I was mad when I walked out with this ponytail,' he said, shovelling pan masala from the palm of his hand into his mouth. 'But even he finally agreed that this was probably the best idea. He didn't want a son who's bald at thirty. It would reflect badly on his age. His own club would probably not allow him in if he got grey hair. Or if he forgot to dye them, rather.'

They had the fixed Wednesday lunch that the restaurant offered. Tomato soup, mutton cutlets and a creamy salad that for some strange reason is always called Russian salad. They talked of, as they say, this and that. A little bit about college, one or two common acquaintances, each other's work. Ajay knew they were sparring, trying to size each other up.

Then, thoughtfully, Yogi made a new and deep opening.

'How's your poetry these days? I remember that in college you were known as a poet.'

'Oh, I gave it up long ago.'

'Why? You should have published a book by now. So many people from our days in the university are publishing books nowadays.'

'Some chance! I don't think I was good enough. Besides, the job that I am in needs a vocabulary of about a hundred words and it seems I've forgotten the rest.'

'Too busy making money, eh?'

'Not doing too much of that either. Just a petty management job. My wife told me when we last had an argument that she was tired of getting five roses, self-packed, every anniversary. I always thought money was not important. But, frankly, now I wish I could make more. Everybody around me seems to be making much more.'

'Get to the market, that's where the returns are.'

'You mean shares and stuff.'

'Yeah, start with some safe issues and see how it turns out. I'll tell one of our boys in the office to give you a call.'

After that, it worked like a charm. As if it had been written all along in small print on the bottle and he had not bothered to read it. Shake well before use, add half a litre of water, shake again, wait to dissolve, and poof—you're rich. After the initial hesitant forays, Ajay quickly gained confidence. Each success made him gamble more at the market. He liked the excitement. He loved to pore over the financial news and the balance sheets. On his office computer he kept details of how every share had moved in the last twelve months. Most of all he liked the fact that he had begun to treat his salary as pocket money.

Life was good. The new car was a small model, but they got it done up so that it looked swanky and smart. It had well-upholstered seats, tinted panes, an air conditioner and a music system with four speakers. In this car, Ajay and Vinita drove around the wide green streets of Delhi from party to party. These were generous, classy summer parties on terraces and in gardens where people drank large glasses of chilled beer and you could vanish into the night when you wanted. At these parties you could meet a young urbane politician, a foreign journalist or the occasional diplomat. But mostly you met young businessmen and their health-conscious wives, well-dressed airline staffers and glib men and women from the advertising world. These people seemed to know all about love and money and the good life. Ajay loved every minute of it. You often got good breaks at these parties. Like the night they met the man with the broad yellow silk tie, who owned a travel agency and gave them a fantastic discount for a weekend trip to Singapore. People were nice to each other at these parties. They didn't mind doing each other favours. In fact it seemed that people went around specifically with the purpose of doing each other favours and chalking it up against the person in their personal accounts for settlement at some later date.

And Vinita got more modelling assignments than before. Recently she had hiked up her fees.

At night, often, they fought. No longer about money. Or children. But there were other things. Like his heavy drinking and the weight that he was putting on. Or the way her photographer friend from the studio kept putting his hand around her waist. Or they fought about nothing at all. Just brooding, growling fights that seemed little more than an expression of the emptiness that had entered their lives.

Like the time they started arguing needlessly while returning from a party late at night. They argued as they parked the car and ran to the apartment block in the rain. They continued to argue in the elevator and as they entered the apartment and began to change for the night. They continued to trade allegations viciously even when they could not recall what had started it all. Their angry shrieks were drowned by the cascading monsoon shower and none of their neighbours heard them. This made Ajay shout even louder but it was a terrific shower and the night outside was black and flooded.

Suddenly he slapped her and even as his palm hit her soft cheek, he realized that he had done this for the first time. It was all over. Perhaps the neighbours, or even the whole world, must have heard the deafening silence that followed. A silence in which the pouring rain did not matter and one could hear, somewhere, the breaking of a twig.

Next morning they were desolate and apart. He didn't know how to look her in the face. But there was a letter for them in the first mail. A bumper issue had awarded them with two hundred shares at a premium. Immediately they were united in celebration. They decided to take the day off, dressed up and went out. Vinita bought a sari from a shiny swanky boutique in a hotel whose lobby had white marble floors and golden chandeliers, where pretty girls hung on the arms of smart young men. At night they went out for dinner to a crowded twenty-four-hour lounge bar. They deliberately went late when they knew it would be full of people. These people would know immediately that Vinita's rustling silk sari had been bought from the most expensive boutique in the city. They would also know the cost of the cigarette that Ajay smoked and the name of the brandy around which he fondly cupped his hands. And both of them felt comfortable. They were among their own kind there.

Forgotten Tunes

Shammi could hear the wheezing of the fat man who stood at the entrance of the brightly lit tent. The man wore a safari suit, tightly and inadequately buttoned across his chest and belly. He was obviously someone from the bride's side waiting for the marriage party to arrive. The importance of the impending moment seemed to make him swell even more and despite the pedestal fan, the sweat poured freely down his thick jowls.

Suddenly the fat man began to move around, flailing his short thick arms. The brass band could be heard turning into the street.

'Cold drinks ready! Get up!' he shouted at the waiters who were still sitting on the dark lawns, tired and lethargic in the heat. Wearily, they dragged themselves up. They all wore frayed black trousers and white coats with metal buttons that had long lost their shine.

The fat man wiped his face furiously and looked around, putting the final touches to all the arrangements. He quickly handed out garlands, straightened chairs and adjusted the fans. Then his eye caught Shammi standing in the shadows. The fat face cut into a snarl and a rough hand pushed at Shammi's throat.

'Get out of here! Beggars! Get out!'

Shammi fell back, clutching the harmonium that hung around his neck on a broad maroon velvet band. His foot got caught in one of the strong ropes that pegged the tent and he fell on the grass.

Something made him sit there for a moment. Perhaps it was the feel of the cool grass through his thin muslin pyjamas. Or the sight of the coal fire in the kitchen tent where the perspiring cook was roasting chickens. Or the smell of marigolds that hung heavy in the still night. Or the realization that this was the first wedding that had taken place in this park in almost a year.

His mind raced back to those crowded weddings of twenty years ago. Then it had seemed that the park had specially been laid out for weddings. It had four large squares of lawn separated by a low neat hedge and a walk tiled with smooth stones. In the centre was a fountain, which could, at a pinch, belong to the festivities in any of the squares. In fact during the wedding season it used to be shared by functions which went on simultaneously in the different squares.

Shammi, his father and three cousins had been a part of those weddings. They had been as essential as the hired tents and the carpets, the gaslights and the fireworks. Singing couplets of love and faith during the nightlong festivities, blessing the bride and the groom and earning a living.

Even though his voice had been shrill then, everybody had thought that he had a way with the harmonium. His father would watch proudly as Shammi's thin fingers would fly over the keyboard and end in a flourish over the low keys. And he would toss his hair back in a flashy motion at the end of each couplet. That gesture had got him the name of Shammi, after a popular film hero.

As he sat on the grass now, he looked yearningly into the kitchen tent. He had not eaten since the morning and it seemed he wouldn't be eating now. Food had never been a problem at those weddings. After the songs, they were always given heaped plates of spiced rice, chicken and cottage cheese with green peas. And large helpings of ice cream for which there used to be an inevitable stampede. Boys in neat clothes would descend from the houses around the park, while their mothers watched from the summer verandas. Such crowds there used to be, thought Shammi wistfully, that nobody ever knew who had been invited by whom. With a sigh he straightened his harmonium and went back to the lights, making sure that the fat man did not see him.

Immediately his hopes rose.

This really seemed like a true traditional wedding. The groom had actually come on a decorated mare. For the last hundred yards or so anyway. The car had been left at the corner of the street and the procession had come in, dancing and drunk. To the house where the coloured lights hung in thick cascades down the front, waving red and green trails through the hedge. Outside the house the procession stopped and formed a circle in which the dancing became more vigorous, then reached a crescendo and abruptly, stopped.

Pushing his harmonium in front of him, Shammi moved to the centre of the welcome ceremony. The bride's father stepped forward with a garland and a humble smile. He hugged the groom's father, who wore a light pink starched turban, one end of which stood out from behind his head like a stiff paper fan. Then the two mothers met and then the two brothers, each trying to lift the other off his feet. A cheer went up and Shammi struck the keys of his harmonium quickly. He was beginning to enjoy himself.

But it ended rather quickly and people moved into the tent, pushing Shammi along. They were greeted with cold drinks, plates of cashew nuts and little vegetarian snacks. Beyond these, Shammi could see the seven-storeyed cake and a mountain of fresh fruit in which an ice elephant was melting rapidly. And the long tables where the food was set out in shiny steel containers, each with a tiny fire under it. Excitedly, Shammi moved to the centre of the tent and sat down on the red and black carpet. The groom, his two sisters and close friends were sitting on the red sofas before him. He tried hard to catch the groom's eye but he was elegantly and with full concentration wiping the sweat from his neck and from under the collar of his white buttoned-up coat.

Then Shammi began to sing. He pumped the harmonium with his left hand and burst into one of his favourite tunes. He sang of the heartlessness of the girl who would not walk to her lover for fear of spoiling the fresh henna on her feet.

But nobody was listening to him. The groom was thirstily gulping down beer from a bottle held by his friend. The guests were pushing each other so that they could be in the frame of the video camera that someone had suddenly produced. The children were running around, throwing flowers at one another and snatching at the cold drinks. A fat foot in sandals kicked the harmonium and the tune was cut off. Two huge sweaty hands clutched at his throat and bodily lifted him up.

'I told you before, get out,' the man in the safari suit was snarling in a low, vicious voice. 'Wretched slum rats.'

And Shammi was on his back again on the cool lawn, tears of anger rushing to his eyes. A boy from the brass band appeared above his fallen figure and took him to where the rest of the band was sitting. Someone gave him a tot of brown rum that was going around. It burnt his throat and his hungry insides. It dried up his tears but it unleashed something else. Closing his eyes he began to sing. The brass band boys smiled, took swigs of the rum and settled back. They took off their shoes and unbuttoned their red coats, baring their chests to the breeze that had begun to leaven the heat.

He sang with all his anger and frustration. He saw the chicken bones pile up in the kitchen tent and he sang with all his hunger. He remembered all the old forgotten songs and he sang with love and joy. And as he drank more of the rum, he sang with all the bitterness that the slum had built up in him, through the lost nights of hunting for food, shelter and bits of happiness. He sang until the brass band got up suddenly, picked up their polished pipes and shining trumpets and rushed off to the entrance to the tent.

The wedding was over. Seven times around the fire. The chanting of mantras, the eternal vows sanctified by the fire and the smell of flowers pressed under the bride's hennaed feet.

Shammi went and stood behind the bridal car, covered with its net of marigold flowers. He watched the bride sobbing into her father's shoulder and he too wanted to cry. Then she clung to her mother and cried like her heart would break. Finally she got into the car where the groom sat, his face drooping and the handkerchief, heavy with sweat, still clutched in his hand. The bride's brothers began to push the car to the end of the street and the band struck up the ancient tunes of separation. Someone began to throw handfuls of coins over the car from a plastic bag and the urchins ran for them. They pushed each other and snatched at the coins among the tired legs of the guests.

Shammi didn't move. 'You're an artist, not a beggar,' his father had once told him, years ago. 'Only take the money that is put on your harmonium.'

As if someone had read his thoughts, two coins spun in the air and landed on the keyboard of the harmonium. He looked down at four rupees and hesitated for a moment. The hunger that he had tried to kill with his songs moved again. He quickly pocketed the coins and pushed his way out of the crowd. Then he was running away from the lights and the flowers. Towards the slum where old Ali's shop behind the bus stop would still have food.

The yellow light from the naked bulb was reflected in the big brass pots that contained the vegetables and the meat. It fell on the shelves of biscuits, sweets and cigarettes and threw into the shadows the pin-ups on the walls. Directly under the lights stood Ali. He was a big, bald man, and the brown sweat trickled down his huge shoulders into his sleeveless vest. His face grimaced as he stoked the coal fire. At last he was satisfied and he took off his vest, wiped his face and shoulders with it, and squeezed it in his huge hands. Then he began to chop onions and green coriander leaves into a pan on the fire. He dipped a long knife into a pan of butter, expertly carved out a thin slice and threw it into the onions. The pan began to sizzle.

Shammi sat on one of the wooden benches that were always put on the pavement in the summer. A small boy in an oversized T-shirt banged a glass of water in front of him along with a plate with some chopped onions, salt and two whole green chilies. Two truck drivers sat on the next table, their legs tucked under them and their turbans beside them. They were eating without a word. Beyond them sat Tara, in a green blouse and orange sari, listening to Ali's gloating voice.

'They took him away today, actually it was only a matter of time,' he was saying, as he ladled curry into the sizzling pan. 'Selling Chinese food in this slum! Imagine! Chinese food from a box on a bicycle! And that, too, without a license. It's not easy. I've been here twenty years. Everybody, even the biggest police officer, knows me.'

With a deft movement of his wrist he moved the pan over the fire. That was true, Shammi thought. Ali had been here forever. Since the time the slum had been a camp of brass band boys, flower vendors and little singers like him. The camp had actually been a child of the park and its weddings. Then the weddings had moved to fancy five-star hotels and the adventurous camp had turned into a vicious slum.

'No Chinese food can take away your business,' Tara was telling Ali, but she was smiling at Shammi. For a moment his hunger wrestled with the clean line of her neck and the dark beauty of her long hair. Then the boy brought the food and Shammi began to eat with the complete concentration that only the poor seem to display when eating. He did not notice the two drivers put on their turbans and start off, with parting leers at Tara. Nor did he notice Tara walking to the counter and curving her thin body around it. She stood there watching him eat, gently tapping one foot so that her anklet jingled. He ate until all the food that his money could buy had finished. Then he got up with the glass of water and went to the edge of the pavement. He rinsed his mouth and sent the water in a jet to the drain. Then he straightened up and looked directly into Tara's kohl-laden tempting eyes.

A creaking staircase led to her tiny room above the shop. A dark green curtain hung on the door. There was a string cot and a stool with a mirror on it. Beside the mirror lay some lipsticks and a can of cheap powder. Over the cot was the framed photograph of a Goddess around which the incense curled in blue wisps.

Shammi had never been there before, but tonight he felt rich. Slowly he gave himself up to the night. He flowed along with it until its silences had drowned out the brass band in his head and its darkness had enveloped all the lights of the evening that had burnt holes in him. When he rose, the sun was already touching the television aerials. He gave his harmonium a parting kiss and laid it gently beside the sleeping Tara. Then, feeling light and free, he took the wooden steps two at a time.

A Certain Thing

The rain fell at a fierce angle on the windscreen. The wiper made clean powerful sweeps but could hardly keep up even though Venu had switched it to full speed. This new model had only one wiper in the centre which made brave grand arcs reaching one end and then having to rush to the other, leaving only the top edges in the two corners untouched.

Venu drummed his fingers on the power steering and decided that he could go no faster, even though he knew every inch of the little road. Anticipating the bends he caressed the steering wheel lightly with his fingers. How this car moved. Just a little touch and the entire monster of black metal, toughened glass and polished steel would respond. The car seemed to be able to see through the rain and the dark, instinctively, beyond the reach of the headlights. Even around the bends, it seemed—its instinctive feelers curving around the clumps of rock and tree and bush.

'Marvel of engineering, this baby,' was how Venu liked to describe it ever since the first time he took it to the Planter's Club. He parked it where he could see it from the bar. The ball boys from the tennis court had crowded around it, like they may have in an earlier time around a captured tiger. The other planters had talked about it, many of them already fixing targets for their next trip to Europe in the summer. Venu had smiled indulgently, jostling the ice in his inch of neat Scotch. His fifty years showed only under his eyes and the way he pressed his knee while getting up from the bar stool.

'It's a loner's car,' thought Venu now as he changed the music cassette. 'Hardly any space at the back, not for people with kids and things.'

His son was at Princeton and only came back once every summer. The other seat in front would do for him. They would take the jeep for the night hunts that his son loved so much. Like that night last summer when they chased a big bull of a deer on the curve after the narrow bridge. A man riding on the bonnet of the jeep had held a searchlight and whenever he could see a movement he would bang the bonnet with his feet. The hunters would then scramble up the hill, chasing the shaft of light. They had got a bullet through the big deer and had to be after him all night. Wouldn't do to let him go injured in an area where hunting was supposed to be prohibited. They had finished him off at dawn and the meat had been distributed among three estates. His son liked the thrill of the hunt, the smell of the wet night and the cleaning of the gun. Venu felt that he would keep coming back as long as there could be hunting in the hills. Princeton was important no doubt. Very important for a career, good for Venu, good to mention at the Club. But it was also important to come back.

Venu crossed the same narrow bridge now. It was made of criss-crossed iron girders. Instinctively he glanced towards the riverbed. Never any water there. Tonight he could hardly even see anything. He accelerated for the curve that he knew must follow the bridge and reached down to flip the cassette. He fumbled and looked down. The car overshot the curve. It seemed to accelerate even more, surprising the darkness totally. A big tree pushed it to the left and it veered away until its right fender hit a boulder. The rain seemed much louder without the music.

They all came to see him in the evenings. Chetti, owner of a cardamom estate, with his left eye twitching incessantly, a large straw hat permanently on his head; Menon, the man who had made his money so fast that nobody really trusted him and everybody wondered what he really did; and Nair, the young and smart one, who had inherited the estate from his father and ran it more like an executive than a traditional planter. They drove up in their vans in the evenings past his bungalow and parked them in garages that were tucked away behind the building.

Venu would receive them in the sunken drawing room. The floor was carpeted in little squares of coir matting and the entire wall was lined with books except where there was a specially designed cabinet for the television and the music deck. The drinks lay on a carved wooden trolley that had one large wheel and two small ones. Every evening Venu would pour himself an inch of Scotch and wait until the others came, a fine grey shawl thrown lightly over the soft cast that cradled his two broken ribs and dislocated shoulder.

'I tell you, this car saved me. It's a marvel.'

The door had taken the force out of the impact and the windshield had not broken. It had caved in but held together in little triangles that broke up the sunlight when they pulled the car out. It had to be sent away for repairs but it wasn't much. Venu didn't write to his son about the accident.

One night after the others had left, he moved into the veranda, leaving the servants to clear away the glasses and plates. The night was falling slowly over the estate and he liked to see the clouds building up. A strong breeze had begun to blow, and far away the sky would light up intermittently. Soon the storm was at his very gate. The sky darkened over and the rain came pouring down. The servants ran out under umbrellas to lock the garages and gates. The rain was falling almost at his feet now, angling onto the veranda. Perhaps he should move in, the cold would not be good for the mending bones.

With a mad rush, Venu's two large dogs charged out from the kitchen door and began to bark ferociously. He could see them circling the old tree that grew in the garden, its old heavy branches curving over the roof of the veranda. As he watched, the dogs kept looking up at the tree and barking. One of them sat down and gave a long eerie howl and then barked again. Maybe a cat is stuck in the branches, thought Venu. There was a loud clap of thunder that drowned out the barking and then rumbled away in waves, reluctantly, like an angry dog pulled away on a tight leash. When it seemed to have almost died out, it rose again. The sky lit up and a vicious bolt of lightning struck the old tree in the garden. A huge branch fell on the roof of the veranda. The dogs were quiet and went back to their shelter, their sides dripping. Venu suddenly felt the chill, and wrapping his shawl around himself, went into the house calling out to the servants to check the damage.

Venu woke up, fumbling for the bedside switch. The clock showed half past four and there was no sign of the morning from the window. He switched off the light and turned over to get some more sleep. But in a few minutes he gave up the effort and went into the bathroom. In the last three months he had hardly ever been able to sleep beyond this hour. A splash of warm water on the face in the yellow light over the mirror. His eyes hurt from the lack of sleep and the touch of water. He ran his hand over his beard: three months of growth. I look different, he thought, another man almost. Feeling a slight sense of satisfaction, he buttoned his warm shirt right up to the neck.

He looked around his room for the sunglasses. Even at that hour he could not think of leaving the room without them. They had become such a habit since the night of the storm. Nervously he fumbled around for them among the books on the table. Books were everywhere in his room. Over the last few weeks, the books from the drawing room had slowly moved into the bedroom. That was where he spent most, almost all his day. Only one servant came in with the food and, occasionally, the estate manager with some cheques to sign. Ah, here they were. The glasses were really dark and even covered his eyebrows. He felt that once he was wearing them he could open his eyes to the world and really look at it. Venu then went out for his only walk in the day.

The hedge around the garden was as old as his beard. Nobody could see into the house easily and the barbed wire would ensure that nobody could get in as well. No one came by anymore. Not since the day that Chetti had driven up and sat without a drink for twenty minutes in the sunken drawing room, waiting for Venu. Venu had not come out to meet him and Chetti had gone away, angry and cursing.

At the club he had told the others: 'He's crazy. I sat for almost half an hour, maybe more, and he was in the next room all the time.'

'What about the servants?' Nair had asked.

'What servants, there's only one of them now. The others were sent off. This one told me that Venu had grown a beard. A beard! And wears dark glasses all the time, even in his bathroom.'

Just fifteen minutes for a walk, that's all. Twice around the compound, twice past the garage where the marvel of engineering lay, all repaired and sewn up like a museum monster waiting to come alive again.

Then he went back to the bedroom and the yellow light came on. He sat on the armchair and the jab of pain rose sharply in the middle of his chest.

He gasped as it rose again, a sharp agonizing wrench that seemed to drag out his life on a piece of barbed wire. He knelt on the ground, his mouth open in a scream. But the servant who came in with a cup of tea heard only a choked weak groan.

The doctor's face swung before his eyes and slowly, like a pendulum running out of energy, came to rest. The doctor smiled. It was a professional, clean smile meant for a patient. Promising hope without commitment. Venu sat up slowly against the big soft pillow, feeling no pain. The room was white and a bright light came from the window. He was without his dark glasses and he could not spot them on the white metal bedside table.

'You got a fright,' said the doctor, the smile still frozen on his face. He was sitting on the edge of the bed, his long bony hands folded over a raised knee.

'Is it a heart...?'

'No, no, we shouldn't jump to conclusions. There's nothing to show that you had a heart attack. There are many similar pains in the chest. You know it could be a muscular pain or just tension. You have been tense I think.'

It was true that he had been tense, ever since that car went off the curve. He needed to take it easy. Maybe he needed to pick himself up, shave off his beard, wear some new clothes and go and have a good drink with the others at the club. They were not his enemies. They would throw parties when his son came back from Princeton the next time. Venu felt a wave of relief sweeping over him. The doctor was not an actor in a worldwide conspiracy any longer. Everything was fine. He liked the warmth of the sun coming in through the window and lay back against the pillows.

'We have to be careful, though,' the doctor carried on, 'and we will put you through the checks. You can rest here a few days. We have a nice garden you know. I'll ask the nurse to give you a shot of morphine so that you can sleep through the first investigation. Looks like you could do with some sleep anyway.'

His smile still in place, the doctor left the room. His rubber shoes crunched and squeaked on the plastic-covered floor of the corridor.

Venu opened his eyes when the young nurse came into the room. She was a local girl who had recently joined the staff. She belonged to a village that was proud of the fact that so many of its girls had become nurses. She was proud of her white uniform and her cap, under which her thick, long black hair was neatly pinned and tucked. She was smiling like all nurses about to give an injection. Venu thought that her face was so gentle, so fresh. He turned his arm towards her and closed his eyes, waiting for the prick of the needle and the tension that would begin to build around it.

But suddenly he opened his eyes and looked at the syringe. Wasn't that too much morphine? Well, she should know. But perhaps she didn't. It did seem too much. Stop, too much, he wanted to say, but a cold hand was already clutching at his throat. She seemed smilingly to inject it forever and he could not stop her. The white walls closed over him with a clean and clinical finality.

The Masterpiece

Last Sunday, I decided to rearrange my books. For me, this remains one of life's unspoiled pleasures which no amount of technology can deprive us of. I dusted them and, sniffing at the yellowing pages, began to put them away one by one. I did not even try to resist the temptation of looking at the dates inscribed under my name on the title pages and wallowing in sentimental reflections. Each date brought back a colour of the sun, the icy drift of a winter or a face. Some drew blanks too, no matter how hard I tried to build a story around them. I finally reached the top shelf which I had avoided for a long time, in fact, many years—I realized this with the inevitable feelings of loss and helplessness that accompany any realization of the passage of time. The shelf contained hardbound textbooks from my law school days. I had never made use of my legal education and had never intended to. But it had been exciting anyway.

As I removed these books, I saw the brown box which lay behind them. Taking it down, I took out the six bottles of oil paint. Each yet unopened, with their blue and white labels intact and the name of the paint company printed boldly on them. The company had once been well known but had not survived the war. I wiped away the dust and set the bottles one by one in the sun on the window sill. The colours seemed as fresh as they had been in those days, twenty years ago...

Those days I had loved painting more than the law, and had given myself to it in whatever leisure I had. With some amount of hard work, I had produced a fair number of canvases. Winter landscapes, mostly. My work had evidently been good enough to gain me entry into a local club of artists and painters. As members of this club, we were allowed to display our works on Sundays in the old market square. We were each given a portion of the wall against which we could lean our canvases. The pencil artists made on-the-spot sketches for tourists for a modest fee and small crowds often collected to watch them. In the summer it was bright and sunny, and the market square used to fill up with cafés. White metal tables and chairs were put out in the sun under colourful umbrellas. People brought their children and ate large ice creams with peaches or chocolate sauce. Or drank weak tea with lots of sugar and slices of lemon in them. During the winter months, the snow lay thick and we could not sit for long as it grew dark early. Sometimes it was too bleak and the wind came up cold from the open expanse of the river. But it was best on the winter afternoons when the sun shone and the bells from the two churches tolled. I was proud to be a member of the club. We even lay down guidelines for what could be displayed in the old square. Abstract art and nudes, except the most artistic ones, were out. I even managed to sell a few canvases during the five years that I sat there, and that was a help.

For things were not easy at that time and I could use all the money that I managed to make. The war was coming on and the shops often did not have things when one needed them. The private traders charged what they thought could be extracted and it was normal to pay extra for all but the most ordinary items. My paints, for instance. For some reason, they had always been difficult to obtain. I used to acquire them only through an old man who worked in a stationery shop. I had managed to cultivate him well enough for him to hide away some for me whenever they came to the shop. He would then hand them over to me for a regular consideration. He liked nothing better than a bottle of rather cheap brandy. After taking the paints, I would present him the bottle with a short speech about friendship and sincere gratitude. He would accept it only after a show of reluctance and some words about how unnecessary it was. For the five years that I bought paints from him, the ceremony never changed.

But then came a time when the shops lay bare and even he could not help me get any paints. Things had changed and it was strange that anybody should be bothering with paints at all. The long queues in the shops were for coffee, sugar and bread and a dark cloud entered our lives. But I did not stop painting, using my stocks sparingly and only for canvases which I thought might sell. I continued my search, but with diminishing hope. Even the visits to my usual source became a mere formality. His discouraging look would tell me to let the bottle of brandy remain in the briefcase. And soon I stopped going to the old market square and began to think of painting as a pastime for which life no longer had any use. And surely, by the time things changed for the better, my best years would be irrevocably behind me.

At that time, and without much hope, I made one more visit to the old man in the stationery shop. He asked me to wait until he finished with the other customers. Then coming to me, he told me in a conspiratorial whisper that he had heard of a woman who had some paints to sell. He passed me an address and I remember noticing even in my excitement that it was one of the new districts near the abandoned airport, which—I had heard—would be used now once again. I began to open my briefcase, as usual, but he signalled it shut. His curious code of ethics probably told him that he had not done enough to earn that brandy and this gave me little hope. He knew, and was honest enough to acknowledge by this silent gesture, that even that cheap brandy was now no longer easy to come by.

I drove out to the new district that very evening. The snow was heavy and it was a long time before I came to the group of five-storeyed buildings which stood like ungainly lighthouses in the white evening. The flat was on the fourth floor and there was no elevator. I went up the poorly lit staircase, past the names on the doors and the pinpoints of light escaping from the peepholes. I shook off the snow from my coat and cap on the piece of sackcloth which lay outside the door and watched it melt as I waited.

The woman who opened the door looked at me in silence.

When I mentioned my purpose, she said nothing but nodded me inside. The flat was dark and small, even smaller than we have them nowadays. She led me into a room where she obviously had not been sitting and lit a couple of candles on the mantelpiece. I sat on the armchair, uneasily. I could see leather-bound books in the shadows, and a few faded photographs in leather frames stood beside a pipe stand on the writing desk. It seemed a man's room designed more for comfort than after a fashion, and I waited for him to appear. But from the way she sat down, it was clear that there was nobody else in the house.

'My husband was a painter.' The voice was flat and direct and made me look up. 'He died in the fighting in the north last month.'

She pulled her hair into a tight knot. She must be in her mid-thirties, I thought, glancing at her when she wasn't looking at me. A shawl was draped loosely over her shoulders.

'He made several paintings and I think he was very good. There was never any time though…'

I waited, hoping that it would all be worth it. She opened a cupboard and took out a few tubes of oil paint. 'I can give you only these.'

I was disappointed.

'If you have some more, I would be glad to pay extra.'

I realized that it had been the wrong thing to say. The eyes that flashed at me were flecked with dark shadows.

'No, there are no more. In any case, I don't even know how good you are and what you paint.'

These words remained with me as I spent the next few weeks using the paints that she had given me. The winter was passing and the snow began to melt, leaving behind a black slush, to which the pristine whiteness was preferable any day. The news about the war only got more depressing. People began to leave the small coastal towns and villages in the north and sought shelter with friends and relatives in our city. Their presence was a reminder of a creeping reality that slowly squeezed out all signs of joy and happiness from our lives. Everywhere—at coffee houses, offices, street corners—

men gathered and talked only of the war. They said it would be no ordinary war, as if there ever could be such a thing.

When the first touch of green announced spring, I found myself heading out once again for the widow's house. I carried with me a few rolled paintings and a sketch or two. She received me kindly, somewhat to my surprise. The room seemed more cheerful, and before I left that evening I had felt familiar enough to look over the titles of the leather-bound books.

She glanced at my paintings between sips of her lemon tea.

'You should think more about them,' was her only comment. She didn't seem in a hurry to get rid of me though, and talked, for the most part, of her husband.

'He would have been a famous painter, had he not got killed in this wretched war. I would have made sure of that.'

And at the end of the evening, a few more tubes of oils. I visited her a few times during the summer. Each time, I went because I felt it was time to go and show her what I had painted since my last visit. I do not know what I expected. A reward, encouragement or praise. Or just more paints, perhaps. It bothered me vaguely that I was never invited.

She received me with increasing warmth and friendliness on successive visits. She would also make some comments about my paintings or pass them over silently. I began to think more about my work and laboured more. And I was satisfied only when she was.

The war reached a point in the fall when there weren't any two opinions about winners or losers. The enemy was a relentless machine and we consoled ourselves with tales of heroism and bravery even as the bandaged wounded began to return home. Our country would be occupied sooner than anyone had expected. People began to move further south, if they still could. Anybody who hadn't yet joined the army was dissolving into the underground which had already begun to form. I, too, would have to make my choice soon. But still, in a desperate attempt to escape, I painted.

It was in those difficult days that I had a strange dream. In it, I

saw myself receiving a brown box as a gift. The box contained six
bottles of paint, their blue and white labels prominently displaying
the name of the company. I thought I would tell the widow about
it the next time I went to see her.

When I did go, she was preparing to move. Hastily tied packages
lay about the room.

'I'm leaving. They will be here soon.'

She did not say where she would go and I could not ask. The
writing table had been cleared and the books were stacked away in
a corner. I felt a sudden sense of loss as if somebody had cleared
away my room without asking me. There didn't seem to be any
conversation left to make. I had brought along a canvas to show
her, and I unrolled it. She held it where it caught the light from the
candles. For a long time she stood silently and stared at the scene
of heavily clothed people filing out of a rough wooden church and
stepping out into the thick snow. The branches overhead were bare
except for the snow, and splintered the light that came from the
weak, very weak sun. She stared at the painting a long time and I
heard her sobbing quietly. I stayed back in the shadows, a stranger
once again.

Without a word she went into the corridor and came back with
a black leather bag. She reached inside and took out a brown box
and handed it over to me quietly. I immediately recognized it as the
box I had seen in my dream, with six bottles of paint, their blue and
white labels all new, and the name of the company emphatically
displayed on them.

'These were especially dear to him. He was saving them for
his masterpiece.' Her voice, uncharacteristically soft, seemed to be
coming over a wide open space and I could not see her eyes.

And then she tied up her hair in a tight knot and said in a firm
voice: 'You can have them now. I think you can make use of them.'
Her manner was that of one winding up months of work.

I never have been able to recall much of what else happened that
night. I think there was an awkward goodbye and I drove around

for a long time. Perhaps I even lost my way somewhere. I do not remember. In any case, I didn't see her again.

But I could never bring myself to use those six bottles or even open them. I never did feel capable of the masterpiece they deserved.

And so, last Sunday, I removed them one by one from the sun on the window sill and put them back in the brown box. The textbooks on law hide them well.

Brute

Between the time that she was nineteen and the day in late July that she turned thirty, Anjali rejected at least ten good men. By then she had become strong and clear-headed enough to admit to herself that she could have, at a pinch, married any of them. Of course at nineteen, she had beautiful long hair, soft fair skin and all the arrogant allure of youth. When Sunit met her for the first time, on the airy terrace of her father's government flat near the Air Force School, he could not take his eyes off her. All evening he stared at her, rocked back and forth on the wrought-iron armchair and senselessly ate platefuls of salted potato wafers with tomato sauce. And he talked in fast forward, quickly and without punctuation—fearing that a break might induce her to get up and walk away—until the sun went down and the huge incandescent lights of the newly built Nehru stadium lit up the sky.

For many evenings after that, Anjali sat on that terrace, amusedly witnessing Sunit slip hopelessly and helplessly in love. He watched her every move and, mesmerized, hung on her every word. She knew that even when he talked to her father, all his senses were awake only to her actions, her thoughts, her perfume. On New Year's Eve, when they were returning from a noisy party, he stopped the car on a fog-laden flyover near the old church and reached out for her hand. She beheld him in fear and amazement as he begged her to marry him. When she responded only with a surprised silence, she saw tears in his eyes. At nineteen she did not know that even grown-up men of twenty-six, men who have jobs and go to offices and take decisions, can sometimes cry. Instinctively, she squeezed his hand and smiled gently and did not say anything.

And so, in the new year, Sunit kept coming to a sunny winter terrace with bouquets of red roses and bundles full of hope. One day when she, languid and relaxed, opened the door for him, she noticed a strange mix of excitement and anguish on his face. He was restless and could not sit still. Finally he got up from the chair and, hands clasped behind his back, began to pace on the terrace. She knew he wanted her to ask him.

'What's the matter with you today?'

He thought for a moment, took a deep breath and said: 'I've been posted abroad. I'm going to Russia in four months.'

'Well, isn't that what you wanted? That's why you joined the diplomatic service. To go abroad and have adventures in strange, desolate places?'

Sunit was quiet and pensive. When he looked straight at her, she once again saw a strange desperation mixed with a hint of tears in his eyes. When he spoke, it was with a measured and placid intensity which always frightened her. It made everything sound serious and final.

'Yes, but all that was before I met you. Now I cannot imagine the thought of being away from you a single day, not being able to come here to you every evening. I cannot imagine it. I will go mad. Even to think of it makes me mad.'

He was silent for a while and then spoke again, firmly and clearly, as if all the confusion in his mind had suddenly evaporated, leaving only the inescapable conclusion.

'There's no way that I can leave you. I can go only if you go with me.'

For the next four months Anjali said neither yes nor no. Her parents watched anxiously from the sidelines as Sunit pleaded and argued, persuaded and ranted. They knew, even Anjali knew, that Sunit was good for her. He was young and good-looking and had the promise of a bright career before him. She would be comfortable and reasonably well off. And what was more, her mother never refrained from telling her, whenever she got a chance, Sunit really loved her.

When it comes to a crunch in life, love is the only factor that makes all the difference. And, her mother warned her repeatedly, one does not often come across people who really care.

But at twenty, such dire warnings seem unreal. At twenty, the world is still new and full of mystery. Hope and love twinkle in every corner. Anjali wavered and veered; she was alternately ecstatic and despondent. In the morning she wanted to be an enthusiastic, young, diplomatic wife, glittering in snowbound parties in Moscow, and in the evenings she held back, afraid to commit herself, wanting to stay back and do something more meaningful with her life. All the time she was aware of the endless possibilities which life, the long life after twenty, might still offer.

In the end, a mere fortnight before Sunit was to leave, she told him that she was not ready to make a decision and that they could always talk of these things when he came on leave the following year. Meanwhile, she told him, in her most sensible, gentle and firm way, that he should go abroad without feeling tied down to her. Sunit was devastated but knew he could do no more except go away and wait for his home leave. He brought her a two-week-old German shepherd pup for her birthday that was still a month away.

'I've named him Brute. He'll remind you of me all the time,' he said melodramatically and, two days later, left on an early morning flight.

Brute grew with surprising speed and, by the time it was winter again, showed all signs of becoming a handsome, strong, huge black and tan dog, in keeping with his unmistakable pedigree. Sunit's letters, two a week, always asked after him. Anjali kept all those letters, with their thick black handwriting and blue and red airmail envelopes, in a round metal box that had the picture of a white, furry cat on its lid. She always kept the lid tightly shut, as if to keep locked in the fierce intensity of the letters in which Sunit shared with her the struggles of a young diplomat living alone in a strange city, far away from home for the first time. He held up each event of those early days for her inspection. His careful selection of a second-hand car, his first real music system, his difficulties with the language classes, the impending exams, his first meeting with the ambassador, and the elaborate preparation for his first real diplomatic dinner at home, were all conveyed for her information, her approval. In those letters there was a plea, sometimes a gentle hint, at other times an impassioned paragraph, that she should be with him through it all. If she were there, it would all be so much easier, so much more fun. In one letter he sent her a large leaf, reddened with the blaze of late autumn, which he had caught as it fluttered down to the Moscow sidewalk. He had written on the leaf—'From Russia with love.' She cried when she got that letter.

She wrote back shorter, more cautious letters, one for every four that she received. Then, as the time of Sunit's home leave approached, she stopped writing. Just a month or so before he was due to return, she wrote to tell him that she wouldn't be in Delhi during his visit, that she was going to Bombay for a training course in hotel management. She wrote that she really had to do this and that she was sure he would understand. He wrote a long desperate letter, made a couple of long, expensive and inconclusive phone calls and then postponed his leave indefinitely. When she came back after three months in a hotel by the sea in Bombay, the flood of his letters had trickled down to one or two a month, and she replied only through a few lines scribbled on the blank side of a New Year greeting card.

Anjali gave herself up to the struggle of making a career in the world of five-star hotels, the world of luxury and comfort, of whispered cultivated tones, rich foreign tourists and tinkling piano notes in white marble foyers. And the underworld of backroom bitching, corporate catfighting and rude, ruthless bosses. It was a world in which one had to be smart and quick and always one step ahead of the others. She was driven by a desire to be smarter than the rest and to move up and ahead. She met many interesting people and a lot of handsome, charming men. A year later she congratulated herself silently on having held out against Sunit's desperate and immature pleadings.

Inevitably there were parties in the evenings which she was expected to attend. Not only attend but also to circulate among the guests, talk to them and always, always charm them. They were all important people who represented business for the hotel, present or future. And ultimately her success would be measured by how much business she got for the hotel. And late at night the hotel car dropped her home, her sari still fresh, her hair still in place and her feet sore from standing too long in high heels. At home she would find Brute waiting for her near the front door, uncomplaining and devoted, his tail wagging. Happy that she was back, even if late, he would settle down on the rug beside her bed, take a deep breath and fall contendedly to sleep.

Her success was no longer in doubt when, within two years of joining the company, she was appointed as the guests relations manager. The appointment brought more responsibility, more work, more parties where one had to smile continuously. She became careful with that smile. It was beginning to bring very tiny, scarcely noticeable lines to the corners of her eyes. Her skin needed more fresh air and expensive care. She began to go for early morning walks with Brute in the Lodhi gardens. She saw how Brute enjoyed those forty-five minutes with her every morning, forty-five minutes alone with her without phone calls or friends. He would rush out of the car excitedly and it took all her strength to keep him on the leash for the first few minutes. Finally he would settle down and walk proudly at her side on the concrete path. And inevitably as they came back to the car park, he would nuzzle up against her leg and look up in grateful devotion. She would just have to bend down and put her arms around his strong neck.

Once in a while, those endless parties in the hotel banquet halls would throw up a man who wanted to know her better, and if he persisted and if he appealed to Anjali, he would be invited home. One summer there was Ronny, who came and nursed many drinks in the low lamplight of her tastefully done up drawing room. All the time Brute watched him from behind the large cushions on the ground; his head was resting peacefully on his front paws but his golden brown eyes followed every move that Ronny made. And when Ronny stopped coming, unable to fathom Anjali's mystery, there was Raminder, the intense young journalist with the constant fire in his dark eyes. One day he too left her cozy drawing room intelligently, shrewdly and quietly, never to return. Then there were several others but there was always something missing, something which Anjali could not put her finger on. Brute watched them all come and go. They all remarked that he never barked. Yet he never let any of them come close enough to pet him; a low guttural growl kept them all at an arm's distance.

When she was twenty-eight there was a quick and silent move in the back rooms of the hotel that resulted in her transfer to the housekeeping department. An inevitable glance in the mirror, and she understood—guest relations needed a younger person. Not required to attend all those parties any longer, she began to spend more time at home, reading and rubbing her feet in Brute's thick fur as he slept on the carpet. If she got up to get herself another large mug of tea, Brute would wake up instantly and watch her every move with an unblinking gaze. Sometimes, when she noticed his gaze she would think of the way Sunit's eyes had followed her every move on an airy terrace many years ago.

When, just before her thirtieth birthday, she met Bharat at a friend's party, she was ready for him. Everything about him attracted her. His man-of-the-world air, his experience, his control, his restraint. He was obviously a man who had seen life.

A few days later, after dinner in an old Chinese restaurant, he told her that he had been married once, briefly, fifteen years ago. But his young wife had died instantly when he had lost control of the car in the rain and crashed into a huge tree trunk. Anjali felt that she could live with the deep shadows in his eyes and with his faraway, haunting, sad memories. She knew that she could put her head on his chest and let him take care of her.

When they came back to her house after dinner, it was still early in the summer night. Anjali threw open all the windows as they settled down in the drawing room. There was a hint of coming rain in the air and insects buzzed noisily against the wire netting of the windows, eager to get to the light inside. The smell of jasmine hung in the air along with the lilting tune of an old film song.

Anjali sat in her favourite armchair near the windows and Bharat sat on a cushion on the ground, his head near her knee. Brute sat across the carpet in the corner of the room, his head up and eyes alert, listening to the buzzing of the insects.

Bharat reached out, held Anjali's hands in his own and gently kissed them. Then, softly, he asked her to marry him. Unhesitatingly, Anjali bent down and whispered in his ear that she would. The next day if he so wished.

For a blessed moment there was complete silence, as if the old film song and the buzzing of the insects had been silenced magically. Then with one strong motion of his large body, Brute leapt across the room. His front paws pushed Bharat deep into the sofa and his strong, sharp teeth reached for his neck. Anjali let out a sharp scream and tried to pull him off. But it was only when she grabbed the dog's leash and whipped him sharply across the face with it that she managed to get him to release Bharat. Brute gave her one long look which made her realize that it was the first time she had hit him, and left the room.

Anjali took Brute with her when she moved in with Bharat after their marriage; it was one of her conditions and Bharat really didn't have a choice. Brute found a corner for himself under the staircase and refused to enter the living quarters. He slept there every night for the one year that he lived after the marriage.

Her friends told Anjali that a healthy German shepherd should normally have lived much longer.

Half Way Home

He has rung up Amita, rather tentatively, to ask if he could stay a day or two at her house when he comes to the big city already wrapped in its early European winter. Not surprisingly, she does not come to meet him at the airport. It was not that sort of a thing. She doesn't even give him a cheek to blow a kiss by as he steps in from the front door of her apartment, down a long, narrow, blue-carpeted corridor from the elevator. She continues to stand at the end of the dimly lit passage, lined with oversized shelves loaded with books. She waves him in from where she is standing as if she had only met him a few hours earlier, not as if she was seeing him for the first time in six years. Years in which he hardly ever wrote to her, and once when he ran into her unexpectedly in a café above the bookshop in Khan Market during her annual trip to India, he had, quite uncharacteristically, been in a hurry to get away. But none of that has made any difference and now he recognizes everything about her as he stands at her door, even her feigned disinterest and distracted smile; it is her old, familiar greeting. In her own way, she has let him know that he is welcome, a friend of long ago in need of shelter and solace.

He is aware of the paintings, dark shadowy profiles on the walls and framed sketches, hung too close, waiting their final placing perhaps in a larger house, as he walks towards her, following her into the kitchen. It's a very white kitchen, hospital clean. Two crystal glasses angle spectrums of a low hanging light as she opens a flat, white fridge fitted deep into the wall, and pours out chilled white wine.

'You need this, I think,' she says, 'but only one glass. It's a Sauvignon Blanc, one of the best.'

Set free by the wine, he stands in the crowded living room, amidst bearded ancestors framed in carved silver, from both sides of a marriage that he hardly knows. He does not want to look around the room; he keeps his eyes averted from her bric-a-brac of a life with somebody else. Neither of them seems to want to talk too much. But he is aware through his fatigue of a darkening glass window, of the spreading tops of old horse chestnuts outside, of old buses adrift in a large city and the occasional youthful voice from the street that seems to break through everything.

Through all the sadness and hurt and defeat and the unspokenness of it all.

He wonders if they all think him terribly old.

'Have to go there,' Amita had said. 'All of them are my friends and we meet once every week, always in the same restaurant. They are all very young, but they like me, I think.'

They all certainly look very young to him, all the fresh, eager faces along the long table in the Middle Eastern restaurant— Lebanese or Turkish or Egyptian. A smudged large mirror on the wall shows him what he already knows, that he has dark circles under his eyes and that his beard is no longer a week-old stubble. He used to shave closely every morning, sometimes twice a day, but now for more than a month it has seemed the most useless chore so he hasn't bothered. It didn't seem to matter, not to anyone anymore.

Even as he stares into his inch of very good whisky, he can see from the corner of his eye the long-legged, long-haired girl next to him kissing deeply the boy on her other side. When she turns back he can feel that she has become aware of him. Pushing back her hair with her long fingers, she becomes an instant confessor with her first glance: 'I am going to break up with him this weekend,' she whispers. 'We will stay together till then. It will be our ten-month anniversary of being together, this weekend.'

Ten-month anniversary. He did not know people kept count of things like that, not in his generation anyway. And he had even taken a twenty-year marriage for granted, foolishly certain even as he gambled with it that it would not go away.

He doesn't ask the question but the girl carries on, whispering: 'No, I will tell him tomorrow. But I know what he will say—best thing that could have happened, he'll say.'

Across the table is a lightly bearded, sensitive-looking boy, a poet by the look in his eyes and the edginess in his manner, constantly fondling the folded bike that is leaning against the wall. 'That's my eternal date, never stands me up. Basil the Brompton.'

He smiles without much meaning. He is with the group without being engaged with them. He envies them their youth, their innocence, the importance that they now attach to things that will later seem so inconsequential. And he pities them at the same time, because they are making decisions that they think will be forgotten by the next summer, unaware that the echoes will follow them into old age. There is nothing that he can say that will save them.

The second whisky and the strong Turkish coffee unpeel something. For the first time in weeks, he seems to step out of himself. The world suddenly seems a wider place, a place where a late night phone call from one particular person or its absence does not make all the difference. Intense conversations that never seem to go anywhere except in circles of guilt and anger and hurt are not the only conversations in the world; there are also chance conversations between complete strangers; there are also frank whispers, honest and true, in which a girl whom he has just met can tell him what she is yet to tell her lover. He is glad to be a stranger, not involved, not accused and not judged. At that time of the night it all makes sense and he is thankful for it.

And across the table from the far end, Amita is watching him, dark-eyed, uncaringly caring; even as he watches her lips speak and smile at someone else.

The guest bedroom belongs to Amita's daughter who has now gone away to college. It has her large teddy bear on the sofa in the corner and some of her high-school books on the shelves. He had forgotten to draw the curtains at night and when the early sunlight wakes him up he still has the tangy taste of orange peels on his lips. He shuts his eyes and turns away from the light and tries to go back to the dream of the familiar second-floor room in Delhi. It is a room in an old narrow house made in the early sixties, accessible only through a round, swirling staircase. A room with a large cooler that wafted a sweet smell of khas in the summer afternoons. A small room, shaded and cool, with an old gramophone, a peacock blue carpet and from somewhere, the sound of water. It had seemed just right for him and the one with the tangy skin once a week, and sometimes twice, when he could get away from his work and his wife. The night's dream had been very complete, down to the suffusion of peacock blue and the awareness of the yellow heat that hung outside, enfolding the long brown pods of the amaltas tree that almost reached the second-floor terrace. During the summer evenings, they would sit in old cane chairs on that terrace, their bodies lazy after making love, drinking gin or beer, listening to jazz that seemed to float away into the dusk. The room seemed completely different in the winter afternoons. The terrace soaked up the sun and the tangy smell of orange peels would soak in from his hands deep into the skin of her neck. But in the dream he has seen no face, only felt her presence, and the texture of her flesh and the scent of a forbidden skin.

He forces himself to open his eyes and look at the brightly lit window. This is the only way of driving the image out of his mind. That dream was the life he had lived for two years. A melange of happiness and guilt, passion and accusations, tears and laughter. And he has now left it behind, because they had come to a point that the room and stolen afternoons could no longer be part of his life. Their destinies, having allowed them a few hours every week, had begun to pull them back home, their respective homes. He had realized that the room with the terrace and the amaltas tree was an escape from his life but it was not his life. And she had not known how to come to terms with his realization.

He gets up, washes his face and goes to join Amita who is waiting with the tea tray, listening to news of the oncoming recession on the television.

The duck pond by which he waits for Amita to come by ripples in the chilly breeze of early November. There is a sun halfway towards a low noon position, weakly climbing. It does nothing to break the chill. He doesn't mind. The ducks walk past the rough wooden table, making rhythmic strutting noises. Late autumn leaves float down into the pond beyond from the horse chestnuts. He reads his own book, tries to select sections that he must read the next day, in a hall where stern portraits of generals and noblemen look down from under arched eyebrows at the audience; and outside, in the hospital lawns, old pensioner soldiers walk around in tweeds, or smoke cigarettes on benches or putt carefully on a green. They live there, he will be told, in exchange for their pensions but only if they have no 'encumbrances'. He tries to select the appropriate sections, those which are dramatic, those which are more or less self-contained, those which will not require too much explanation. And he wonders: did I really write this book? When? How? How did he drag out this story from those two years which were pure passion and dark despair all at the same time? Once in a while a memory of unmatched bliss tries to walk in into his consciousness but is dragged back by some burst of accusation, some horrible feeling of inadequacy. But he did write it and that is the reality under those horse chestnut trees. His finger tries to feel the print on the page as if it were Braille, and he can feel the book's weight in his hand.

Two women carry their coffee cups to the next table. Then they get up again to bring their hot crêpes with chocolate sauce from the counter. He can understand their conversation—he realizes that even before he realizes that they are speaking Russian. It takes him back years, to a landscape when everything was fresh and young, when the questions were not so harsh. By such a pond in Russia his two-year-old son was photographed half covered by rust red autumn leaves, a blue plastic shovel in his hand. That was a precious photograph and he wonders where it is, in which album, lying in which cupboard of the house. And he wonders, too, where all the years went and if he had them again, what he would have done.

But he knows even as he wonders that he would have done all the same things all over again, the good and the bad, because at no stage did he really have a choice. And even as he says that to himself he wonders, too, whether it is just one more weak justification.

Amita, on her way back from office, meets him by the pond and they take the longer of the two tracks around the park. It seems more like a collection of soccer fields; he can see many sets of goalposts, painted chalk white. The cold only bites him occasionally, on the back of his neck above his jacket collar when the wind picks up, and he is glad for it. It keeps him in the present and that is where he wants to stay. He knows if he stays there long enough things will begin to improve.

They step into the orangery that is hidden away in one corner of the park. There is no fruit on the trees but the view from the table at the corner is pleasant, right up to the skyline of spires and domes. The coffee is slow, strong and long-brewed, the way he likes it, and the carrot and walnut cake is not too sweet. Over the coffee and the cake they trade stories that don't really matter. He knows that she wants to ask questions and he wonders what he will say. But ultimately she lets it be.

Once in a while he looks out through the glass sheets with their black metal frames at the view outside. The colours from the vaulted museum they have been to in the morning have still not left his mind; the pictures float and he lets them. It doesn't take much effort. Van Gogh's sunflowers outshine the rest; he can feel their blaze against the back of his eyes. And like the tour guide that they overheard, he too cannot make out the exact colour of Cezanne's bridge in the Japanese garden that now seems to stretch across his imagination. Was it white or brown or green or blue?

Amita does not know where his mind is but she feels that he is looking at the weak sunlight as if for the first time.

'You are coming back,' she says, 'from somewhere, wherever it is.'

'You have to meet a friend of mine,' Amita says, as they walk along a canal, matching steps effortlessly, in and out of the darkness of those short tunnels, past gently wafting white boats.

He is not sure he wants to meet anyone, certainly not anyone new. All he wants is his mind to stop wrestling, even if for a while, with those sleepless questions. Questions which really have no answer, or none that matters. For all that had to happen has happened and everything that should never have started has now been ended. He will never go back to the room with a terrace.

'It'll do you good,' Amita insists. 'You may even know her from somewhere; you come from the same parts.'

The friend is an ascetic thin presence with a narrow face. She is waiting in a café above a sprawling railway station, preciously holding a brown paper package. She opens it to show two coffee mugs with blue and yellow swirls.

'I finally made these today, after a month of pottery lessons,' she says by way of introduction.

'Are you from the hills? Shimla?' he ventures.

'Yes, you have been well briefed. A little beyond Shimla actually, near the last curve near Mashobra bazaar. A green and yellow house.'

It comes to him as if he were standing before it, from all those miles, hundreds of miles away. A yellow cottage with a green roof, wild rose bushes tumbling over the old stone boundary wall, just above the road a steep cemented path leading up to an iron gate under a curved trellis, also festooned with wild roses. He can feel the light filtering faintly through the thick deodar cover. He can see the road, uneven after the ferocity of the monsoon, forking before him. The lower fork will sweep away to Naldehra and beyond, while the upper one will go swiftly into the bazaar, meeting it near the liquor shop, where the monkeys trapeze on electricity wires. In the filtering light he can see himself walking along that road, carefree, trusted and trusting, in the days before the cheating and the lying. He looks up gratefully into the narrow face with the grey penetrating eyes and feels a warmth which he hasn't, for a long time. He recognizes it as the warmth of a homecoming.

But the friend's attention is elsewhere. A man has hailed them across the café and soon they have joined two tables and are all sitting together, sipping cappuccinos with chocolate swirls in the milky froth. The man—he catches the name of Foster in the short introductions—is about sixty, nattily dressed in the manner of someone who has spent his life in the tropics, doing strange, secret things. He wears a beaten leather coat and khaki-coloured corduroys, and a knitted scarf is tucked into a check shirt. Next to him is a child of about ten or eleven, with Eastern features and a smooth brown complexion, a large milkshake before him.

'He is the son of my Thai girlfriend. I promised her I would bring him up. What do you do?' Foster asks genially.

He hesitates a moment and then he says: 'On long leave from the Foreign Office. Have been doing some writing.'

'Ha! The Foreign Office. Spent twenty-eight years for them myself. Hated every minute of it.'

'That's a long time to hate something,' he says before he realizes with a start that this month has seen the end of twenty-eight years for him too, a different Foreign Office, a different government, but the same number of years of being jostled around, not knowing where he would be a month later, the same excitement, adventure, strange conversations in distant bars, the tinkling of crystal glasses, the minutely written notes, the reading between the lines…twenty-eight years. He likes Foster, perhaps because of the loyalty he has shown to his Thai girlfriend of long ago.

Then he looks at Amita who has been quiet all afternoon, letting things just happen, watching the trains slide in and out of the station. Why are these people meeting me, this friend from Shimla, this man with twenty-eight years in the Foreign Office, he seems to ask. Why are these coincidences happening…when I did not even want to meet anyone?

Amita begins to talk in the train. They are sitting next to each other, shoulders barely touching. Like they used to sit in the Bombay suburban trains thirty years ago, when they were lucky enough to get a place, their cotton bags youth protest badges in themselves, full of books on philosophy and politics. That mere touch of the shoulders could feel like an embrace. Now he can barely bear to touch anyone. He has been scalded by flesh; he has felt the fire of obsession in those summer afternoons. He has seen how the shine of a collarbone under pale skin, the throbbing blue vein in a wrist, the slow arching of a foot, can change everything, destroy all resolve, make it all worth it and then destroy it all again.

'I do not know where you have been,' she is saying. 'You are not ready to tell me, not yet, though one day you will and then you will be cured. But I know where you are going, you have already decided though you do not know it yourself: you are going home, where you belong. And my purpose is only to help you on your way, to smoothen your transition between two worlds. That is my destiny; you were never meant to stay with me. But only this time you ventured too far afield, you could not return straightaway, you would have destroyed yourself and others in the process. These three days were meant to happen. You had to come by me; you had to meet all these people. Each one, even I, had been placed where we were destined to meet you on your way back, to push you along. In a way, nothing was a coincidence. Now go.'

Rumki

Wrapped in blankets against the fresh cold of the evening, Chandgi Ram and I sat, hunched low on a string cot outside the hut that was to be my home for a month. It was getting dark but the stars over the inky blueness of the hills below us were bright. Otherwise there was not a single light to be seen. Jakhna was twenty miles away from the little district town that lay around the shoulder of the mountain. At the little town there were some offices, and a couple of buses daily disgorged their loads of dusty travellers, dizzy from their long ride along the twisting road into the interior. At the little town too, two roaring mountain streams met to form a river that would go on, many hundred miles later, to feed a plain and be worshipped and feared.

But Jakhna was very far away from all this. Perhaps this was the reason that my visit had been treated with so much importance. Even though I was a trainee, I was probably the only official who would be staying in the village for more than a few hours. Besides, I was supposed to know about all the things that mattered—things like the law, electricity, fertilizers and the police. It had been written all over the faces that had welcomed me on my first evening in the village. They had followed me in a group, as I had bent carefully under the specially erected gate of broad leaves and yellow marigold flowers. Their silent eyes had scrutinized every move of mine as I washed my hands, sat down and sipped the sugary tea. They would have stayed there all night if they had not been chased away by Chandgi Ram, the local keeper of land records.

'Go away, all of you now, he has to rest.'

When they had gone, reluctant but obedient at his urgings, he himself stood patiently in the corner waiting for my first sign of approval. When I had finally asked him to come and sit down, he had walked out of the corner, softly, wearing an unctuous smile. He had immediately held out a large register in which he, and before him his father and grandfather, had carefully mapped out the village landholdings in minute, black, unquestionable detail. Ever since that night, Chandgi was constantly at my side, his register clutched under his arm as if it were a natural extension of his body. He would be waiting for me as I would step out of the hut on foggy mornings and would lead me from house to house in the village until the sun was high up in the sky.

'That's Sadhu Ram's house. He was given a plot in 1971 under the Programme of Land Gifts.'

'Does he cultivate it himself now?'

'Yes, when we have rain. He is all right now.'

'And water, from the river?'

'One tap, sahib, and the pipeline is twenty miles long.'

'One tap for the whole village...?'

And when the sun rose very high in the sky, we returned to lunch and rest. At night, Chandgi would wait until I had eaten and would then silently melt away, but only after he was certain that I needed nothing more.

But for now he sat and smoked one of my cigarettes. He puffed at it with a certain dignity and held it so that only the red smouldering tip showed out of the end of his fist. All around us, the smoky wintry smell of burning cow dung had fallen like an invisible cloak and Jakhna seemed all set to vanish into the hills for the night. There was a hurried step near us and we looked up. A young girl, her head covered, was walking up the path that led past the hut. She passed us and glanced up. I caught the look. It was a brief straightforward look, brave and fearless. Rather like a tigress surprised when roaming the jungle at night. Then she was gone but her large eyes, set in her thin dark face, bright even in the darkness, troubled me.

'Rumki, granddaughter of Bayi Ram,' Chandgi had anticipated my question.

'Parents?'

'Her father was a drunkard. I saw him only once, years ago. She's always lived with her grandfather. Bayi Ram is a good man.'

A dark cloud rolled up from the valley very slowly, until it had eclipsed the bright stars over the lower hills. Chandgi Ram slowly retreated. I sat on until it became palpably chilly, and then reluctantly returned to the harsh yellow light that hung in the hut.

It was a couple of days later that Chandgi Ram led me to Bayi Ram's hut. Like all the other huts, it was built on two levels. On the ground floor there was enough place to store firewood for the entire winter. A goat was tied to the rickety ladder that led to the second level. I had to bend low to enter the narrow wooden projection that served as a veranda. I could see that Chandgi had done the rounds in the morning, warning Bayi Ram of my impending visit, for a narrow mattress covered with a blanket had been laid out in the veranda as my seat. Chandgi seated himself on the far corner of the mattress while Bayi Ram sat on his haunches with his hands folded, watching carefully as Rumki brought the tea. It was sweet and heavy with goat's milk.

Chandgi watched the girl go inside.

'What's with her father?' he asked.

'Drunken wretch. He's gone. Forever, as far as I care.'

The old man spat over the ledge behind him.

'He came, he came once, maybe three years ago. Just threatened me and went away.'

'What do you plan to do with the girl?' I asked.

The old man was silent.

'Maybe,' I continued, 'you could send her to the Centre. I hear they have someone there who teaches girls to stitch and to tailor.'

'It is far, sahib. She must get married. I am waiting for Jai Chand, Pali Ram's son.'

I looked at Chandgi Ram.

'Jai Chand works as a cook in a restaurant in Delhi. Many of our boys work as cooks but they say he is the only one who makes Chinese food. God only knows where he learnt to do that. But there is good money in it.'

'He will come in the summer,' the old man carried on. 'I've spoken to Pali Ram already.'

Then we had more of the sweet, heavy tea. The sun shone brightly and just sitting there with my back resting against the wall made me drowsy, and I thought vaguely about Rumki tinkering around the hut and her future as the wife of a cook of Chinese food. Chandgi Ram, with a flash of the sharp understanding that had no doubt made him and his ancestors custodians of power in this straggling little village on a remote grey hillside, suggested quietly that we should call it a day. I agreed and climbed down from the hut. It was not much of a village anyway and if I worked too hard I would hardly be able to justify my month's stay. So I took it easy and slept through the afternoon.

Nevertheless a month is after all a month and it began to pass rather quickly. The next day that I clearly remember was my last Sunday in the village. It was full of drama. Early in the morning Chandgi Ram knocked on my door and brought in the carpenter. The man was nearly in tears. He was not being given sugar by the local dealer and his daughter was to be married in two days' time.

'We have so much to cook, and there *is* sugar in the shop... He sells it for a profit, that's what he does.'

We called the dealer and he agreed to give some sugar. Of course he made his excuses and accused the carpenter of having taken sugar just two weeks earlier.

Then Chandgi Ram returned again just before lunch, an excited flush on his face.

'Not good thing happened, sahib.'

'What now, Chandgi?'

'You remember, sahib, you remember Rumki, Bayi Ram's granddaughter?' Even in his excitement Chandgi would not name a person without giving the name of the person's father or guardian. 'We have been to their house, there below the shop.'

'Yes, yes, I remember, but what is the matter?' I could feel my own excitement mounting.

'I was walking past just coming to see you when I saw her father, that drunkard whom I haven't seen, I don't know, for maybe seven years now. He was going up to Bayi Ram's hut so I just stopped to see what would happen. You know it is good for me to know what's happening because then later they always come to me for help.'

'Go on, what happened?'

'There was a lot of shouting. It was him shouting for the most and I am convinced that he was drunk and that, too, in the afternoon. I think basically he came to take Rumki away, said he wanted to get her married off as she was now grown up. And he shouted that he had been promised five thousand rupees for her. Five thousand rupees, he shouted and I think some people must have heard. Not good.'

Chandgi sat down, then saw that I was standing and he quickly jumped to his feet again.

'And then, that Bayi Ram also shouted back at him and came out of the hut with his stick. Who would think that the old man still had the strength to even pick up such a heavy stick? He hit him on the head. There was blood, and when that wretched fellow had come down the ladder, Bayi Ram followed him and hit him again. But it's not good, not good. Bayi Ram is old, very old and his son shouted that he would come back.'

'But Chandgi, can't we do anything?'

'Do what, sahib? What can we do, he's the girl's father.'

'But he can't sell her for five thousand rupees!'

'It's a lot of money.'

It was my last week, so I stopped going around the village. I would pull out a little table and a chair into the sun and work on my report. There was much tabulation of statistics and I wrote my conclusions and suggestions. I worked to make it look neat and impressive, though even then I remember wondering whether it would be read at all. Perhaps somewhere it would help in bringing more drinking water, or electricity or even a primary heath centre to the village. Or perhaps it would be bound with ten similar reports and be catalogued away in a library.

It was on one of those days that Bayi Ram came to see me. The sun had become too sharp and I had moved my table near the wall of the hut so that only my legs were out of the shade. The old man came up and sat down on his haunches. He looked very old indeed and as he sat the knobbles of his knees stood out like large marbles.

'What is the matter, Bayi Ram?' But even as I asked I got the feeling that it was something terrible.

'Rumki, sahib, she's gone. He took her away.'

'When?'

'She went to get water from the tap as usual this morning. She didn't come back. The drunken wretch, I curse the day he was born.'

Early morning. A blue, cold, breezy morning. Alone at the tap. A tune rises in her head as the water falls in jerky bursts into the bucket. Water that has coursed through twenty miles of a blue, grey mountain. Summer would come and Jai Chand would return. The sun is already nearly up and the tune in her head is insistent today. Just then, an ugly face rises in the cold; vile eyes and a bushy, grey moustache. A curse, a scream, five thousand rupees. A blanket over her face and she's made to walk and walk. Maybe that's how it happened.

'Do something, sahib, if you can.'

Two days later, my month in Jakhna came to an end. Chandgi Ram seemed sad as he helped to put my bag into the jeep. I drove away, downhill and across the face of the mountain until I came to the little district town. I crossed the bridge where the two streams met. They had been building a dam there for the last twelve years. When it would be ready, the entire town and the villages and the trees would sink. I filed a report about Rumki at the small police station which also served as a post office. Then, quickly, I drove away, past many villages, not daring to guess in which of them Rumki was married.

Barrier Beach

As I boarded the midday ferry to Martha's Vineyard, the vicious knot of hurt and despair I had carried in my heart for so long seemed to escape into the bowl of a grey overcast sky. From there, once again, it descended upon me, the boat, the water and the two edges of land, like the collective sorrow of the whole world. It seemed impossible to roll it back into myself again. The battle was lost, and I wanted to sit down, put my head in my hands and cry.

The black bag with my sketchbook, a bottle of water and spare shoes had begun to cut into my shoulders. I took it off and used it to cushion my back against the wall of the cabin. The cabin hid me from the direct blast of wind and the sight of dozens of tourists choosing and changing seats on the open deck, as if this was not a forty-five minute journey but an endless pleasure cruise. Here, I thought, I could be alone, alone with my tortured thoughts and memories; I could once again unravel and bind, and relive the bittersweet pain, much like a man who will repeatedly probe a bad tooth. Sitting there, I watched a few gulls as they rode the wind along the boat, bravely, adventurously, like heralds in a line. Then at some unseen, unheard command, they cut away and fell sideways in a clean slice from wind to water. I envied them their ease and grace as they cut away. They left no blood, no jagged edges, no untidy knots.

She came from the other side of the deck and turned to the protection of the cabin wall to light a cigarette. Leaning back, her head and the sole of one foot rested on the wall as she smoked. I noticed the brown roundness of her legs. Her short dress, a darker brown, thin for the hot day, fluttered as she held it down occasionally with a thin hand to her thigh. I half resented her intrusion into my private corner. Once, or twice, I tried to see her face but it was hidden, mostly by a large straw hat and brown, thin, long hair. Only a large, colourful handwoven Indian bag on her shoulder was an exception to the shades of brown.

I waited for the crowds to leave the boat and savoured the emptiness of the deck as we touched land. Several boats lay in the shallow water of the little harbour, their masts motionless and straight, all in a line. It was an abandoned graveyard of unclaimed boats, and it pleased me to see them at rest. This way they were predictable and their reflections were still and perfect. I was sick, deep down, of sudden whims and chance decisions; I yearned for a world of true angles and perfect reflections.

The ramp was clear and the people who were to board the ferry for the journey back fumed impatiently. They were done with Martha's Vineyard. It had been ticked off the checklists of their lives and they couldn't wait to get on to the boat and go back to their cars, drive to their suburban villas, send their kids to school and mow the lawn every Saturday morning. I envied them the predictability of their lives.

I saw her again at the bike rental shop. She had taken off her straw hat. Her dark brown hair flew in the wind as she struggled with a bright blue biking helmet. Like me, she had shunned the air-conditioned bus tour and like me, again, she had walked past the open trolley bus which would go through four towns and stop at Edgartown for an hour and a half. Like me, I thought, she wanted to be alone and feel the warm wind and the sun on her face.

It felt good to be cycling again. It felt nice to be doing something that I had convinced myself I would never be able to do without Nina, and if I dared to do it I would be torn asunder, picked up, flung back to the ground, lifeless. It was a myth, our holy togetherness; and that myth too was now gone. I was alone and free, sadly. Only the narrow trail along the blue sea in a straight line, an ancient lighthouse in the distance and far ahead, a rider in a brown dress and a bright blue helmet.

Sometimes you know that some things will happen. I knew that I would catch up with her and talk to her. It was as if everything else, the ferry, the island, the weather, the low-flying gulls, the cycles were all stage props for this one central act. I had felt this certainty deep down in the bones of my forearms only twice before in life: once when I met Nina in a college café and once when she was about to leave the house, with her suitcases and her paintings, two months earlier. Each time the inevitability of coming events, the knowledge of a greater destiny taking over, had made me fearless, careless.

Carelessly I stood my bike next to hers at the seafood place near the jetty with the three boats. Fearlessly I took the chair at her table on the wooden deck. The wind came and swept the paper napkins off the table and nearly toppled the beer in my plastic glass. She smiled and threw back her hair. Behind her I could see lonely holidaymakers in little verandas of little toy houses, which looked out over the jetty. Old couples rested in armchairs and pairs of girlfriends, women without men, defiantly swigged beer from brown glass bottles.

I watched her brown, liquid almond eyes. Gently laughing, kind eyes set apart in a not so young, open face. A little scar above the left eye balanced a fine dot of a brown mole on the right cheek. Beads of perspiration formed above the thin, fine upper lip. Drops condensed on the glass of chilled white wine that she held by the stem, straw-coloured wine that made one aware of the lazy warmth of the afternoon.

Since the moment that Nina had walked out at four o'clock that afternoon, leaving an unmade bed, half a cupboard upside down on the floor, mugs of coffee unwashed in the kitchen sink, I had not sat that close to a woman. Alone at the same table, sharing an undefined space, a couple to the rest of the world. I didn't even know her name.

I glanced at the book in her hand. *Selected Poems* by T. S. Eliot, a slim volume with a grey design of squiggles and squares and a thin pen sketch of Eliot. Once in a while she smiled wistfully, as

if an image had by chance touched off a long forgotten memory.
Suddenly she spoke: 'Listen to this:

> *There will be time, there will be time,*
> *To prepare a face to meet the faces that you meet...*

That was the first time I heard her voice. It was thick with a
foreign accent, probably East European.

'Did you prepare your face to meet my face? Was that why you
were cycling so slowly, preparing your eyes, your nose, your ears?'

I did not answer. How quickly one forgets the ways to banter
with women. Nina and I had abandoned light-heartedness a long time
ago. Locked it away in a metal box along with carefully catalogued
youthful photographs and old records that we didn't play any longer.
Spontaneous joy and quicksilver laughter had changed into lines
frozen around our eyes, at the corners of our lips, stretched deeply
across our brows... I wanted to tell her that I knew what she was
alluding to, that I knew the poem and the only question was—do I
dare? That I had known them already, the evenings, mornings and
afternoons, but that I was middle-aged and disillusioned and needed
time to come back to life.

'Don't tell me anything,' she said. 'But if you like, you can cycle
with me.'

As she cycled, she sang from under the wide brim of the straw
hat. I caught the melody whenever I came up to her and lost it
when I had to drop back to make way for joggers coming towards
us. It was a melody from some distant gypsy campfire. I could not
make out the words but I sensed the warm glow of the campfire,
the rhythmic dancing vagabond feet, barren birch trees and cold
shadows beyond the circle where there was snow.

By a campfire at a university, in a huge park that smelt of
honeysuckle and roses, I had held Nina's hand under her heavy
red and black shawl. Our fingers were entwined as she leant on
my shoulder. The fragile smell of her skin, the plastic smell of her
lipstick, the perfume from the hollow of her neck, all of these had
crept into my deepest inner spaces. I was helplessly in love. On

the other side of the campfire, in the dark, was another melody—
someone sang a popular song to the whimsical strumming of a
guitar. I would never have thought so then, but I have forgotten the
face and the words. Twenty-two years is a long time to remember.

We were cycling along the narrow barrier beach and the wind
blew the sand from the dunes and hit our faces and legs and arms
like thin, invisible pygmy arrows. From behind the clouds some bit
of the sun lit up the backwater and the reedy marshes. A magical
late afternoon light fell on the long swaying reeds, a strange red
bird flew low over the water, a few small red flowers lit up the edge
of the high ground that rushed past our cycles. Her strong, brown
legs pedalled fearlessly, carefree. She didn't look back but I knew she
waited for me to catch up, ride with her.

I nearly fell over as she suddenly braked to a halt.

'Look at that,' she said.

I watched an old man in blue shorts combing the beach in the
low water. He bent over, his strong muscular body dredging the sand
with a many-pronged shovel.

'He's searching for shellfish,' I said.

Her eyes squinted against the wind and the light, her one hand
held her hat, the other pulled her dress against her thigh. Under her
breath almost, she quoted:

> I should have been a pair of ragged claws
> Scuttling across the floors of silent seas...

'Maybe he'll find some,' I said.

'Maybe he'll find something else. Maybe he'll find something
he doesn't want to find. One day we were digging like this,' she
continued, 'I and my little brother, with plastic shovels. It was on
a beach on the Black Sea, not one of the main beaches but some
holiday resort where my parents would go every year with other
people from the Institute where they worked. There were lots of
people and we knew everybody around. I kept digging until I had
made a big hole. I found a book. It was a huge red leather-covered
book. When I took it to my father his hands shook. It was a banned

book and in those days in my country, one could be killed for having it. Someone had hidden it away in the sand. We didn't know what to do with it so we put it into a pink plastic bucket, and walked down the beach and dug a new grave for it in the sand. My father was worried for days that somebody may have seen him carrying it and he prepared my mother every day for the moment he would be taken away, constantly telling her where all the papers and keys were kept. But nobody had seen him; nothing happened. Even now when I see a thick leather-bound book, I pick it up and I can feel the grains of wet sand all over its pages. I can feel the paper, soggy and thick, breaking like wet biscuits under my fingertips.

The old man was now out of the water and from across the narrow road I could see him walk, with his shellfish in a bag and the shovel under his arm, to a grey Range Rover. She had forgotten about him. We sat on the pebbles and in silence watched a large boat with sails and masts, standing still in the waters of the Sound. Against a lowering sky it formed an old-fashioned still painting, a modern Cutty Sark. A surfer clinging to a bright pink and yellow sail rushed back and forth across the still scene, like a gaily coloured insect trapped in a bottle. At the edge of the beach, on a rise with a wooden bridge, where the water flowed into the marsh, a few men waited motionlessly near their lines, waiting for the last fish of the day. A brother and sister were skipping flat stones in the twilit water: one, two, three, and finally four. Down the beach, past the little van selling frozen lemonades, a girl in a black swimsuit walked tentatively into the water in the silvery, brittle light. Once in the water she could have been a mermaid singing in the distance at dusk. Her imagined song took some of the sadness out of the sky.

I turned back to her in the brown dress. She was lying back on the pebbles and she was looking at the sky, where a single gull circled and coiled, rose and dipped. A careless cigarette dangled from her hand and the sand stuck to her legs and her bare feet.

'Don't ask me anything,' she said. 'Just watch the sky darken, bit by bit.'

'An artist,' I asked tentatively, 'a poetess?'

'No,' she turned her face fully towards me—'I am a well-read, elegant escort, a very high-class prostitute. I work the bars in Nice, Venice, Gstaad, only the very expensive, exclusive bars. But I am on vacation. Now watch the sky.'

The eight-thirty ferry was cancelled and a big crowd gathered for the next one. There were all sorts of people on the deck in the hot, early night. People with firm skin and people with flab, tired people and people with youth and charm. Silences, bits of poetry, thinly fractured intimacies and half-forgotten wounds floated back to the mainland. We stood in this crowd near the railing and watched the lights on the island grow faint, the wind in our faces.

Sunrise at Mashobra

After the sudden hairpin bend, the guest house in the forest came into sight. Ranjana felt her anger reach out before her and poison the late afternoon sunshine. It split the ancient silences of the endless deodar forests and left screaming echoes in its wake.

'You've been to this guest house before, haven't you?' she asked Shekhar, as the car took the last iron bridge over a gully and bumped up a stony climb.

'Yes, once.'

'I thought so. You were right, too, about the sixteen bridges.'

'You counted?'

'Wasn't I supposed to?'

'What's the matter?' Shekhar looked at her and reached for her hand as the car stopped.

'Nothing,' she replied. Pulling her hand away, she opened the door and got out of the car. Outside, it was colder than she had expected and she was glad that she had brought the heavy jacket with her.

Shekhar led the way to the front of the guest house. Her questions followed him one after the other.

'So now that we're here, what's the routine? What is it that we simply *have* to do here, eat here, see here?'

He turned around and looked at her sharply. But she avoided his eyes and went past him and up the three stone steps to the veranda of the guest house.

Shekhar had never seen Ranjana in this mood. Not once in the ten days since they had been married in a crowded court of a magistrate, amidst a group of friends who complained that an unseasonal November rain had spoiled several pairs of expensive shoes. Nor even in the year that he had known her as a fellow lawyer in the Delhi High Court. Ever since their first meeting a week or so after his divorce from Anita had come through, he had only thought of Ranjana as quiet, soft-spoken, gentle. And loving, he thought, caught unawares by pleasant memories of their nights of love during the last week in Shimla, at Mount View Hotel in room number 52. From the semi-circular wooden balcony of that room, he had loved seeing the sun's first rays reach out to Solan, Dagshai, Kasauli and the hazy plains beyond.

The chowkidar came out to meet them. He was a furtive man with stained teeth, who kept tugging at the knitted dark green muffler that was tied thickly around his neck.

Shekhar spoke warmly to him.

'How are you, Mani Ram ji? Mani Ram, right? All well? I see the guest house is fine, as before. And do you still make your great masur daal and rice and serve it with that great mango pickle. That's what we will have today. And, yes,' as the man turned to go away, 'two glasses, please.'

Ranjana watched Shekhar pull out a bottle of white wine from the leather bag slung across his chest. It irritated her that he had wanted to bring only white wine along, although he himself kept saying that it was the wrong drink for this weather. She had not given the matter much thought at that time but now it bothered her.

The chowkidar came out again. He was carrying two glasses on an octagonal melamine tray with large red and green flowers painted on it. The glasses were tall and ordinary. They would have been more suitable for rum and coke than white wine.

'Sorry,' said Shekhar. 'I'm afraid this place has no wine glasses.'

Ranjana sat silently on the armchair and did not say anything. Her eyes were fixed on a single electric bulb that had begun to shine in a window a little below the guest house. It might be the house where the chowkidar lived, she thought.

Shekhar had opened the bottle of wine in the manner that she had seen before, carefully and with studied concentration. He put the cork gently aside and wiped the bottle with the palms of his hands. Then the last rays of the sun glinted weakly on the straw-coloured wine as he poured it into the two glasses. He picked up one and, bending slightly towards her, handed her the glass.

'Sorry again,' he said. 'It should be chilled but I hope you won't mind, in this weather.'

As if to deliberately scoff at the ceremony he had indulged in, Ranjana quickly raised the glass to her lips. She did not sniff for the bouquet; she did not sip gently at it. She emptied half her glass and put it down on the dark round wooden table before he had even touched his. The wine seemed to seep through her anger and touch something deep within.

When she spoke, her voice was terse.

'What all are you going to be sorry for, Shekhar?'

He looked up in surprise. He had thought that her dark mood had passed.

'I don't understand.'

'Then let me make it clearer. Are you going to be sorry for bringing me to Shimla for my honeymoon? For making me stay at Mount View Hotel, in room number 52? For showing me the same sunrise you must have shown to Anita, over a pot of the same Kangra tea? For taking me on the same walks to Summer Hill, Viceregal Lodge, the same tea at Davicos, the same breakfast at Mehru's? What else are you going to be sorry for?'

Shekhar was quiet. He leaned back in his armchair and placed his open palms over his eyes. Strangely detached, Ranjana stared past his shoulder, past the wooden railing of the veranda, past the valley below the guest house, at the distant edges of a hill beyond which a reluctant sun was going down. A smoky sadness had risen from somewhere, from some lonely cooking fires in the valley perhaps, and entered the soul of the evening. It seemed to float around, wrapped in a nameless nostalgia and then, almost as if by mistake, descended exactly where they sat.

Shekhar knew that Ranjana was right. It was no use protesting. From the lunch at Stag Café, a few miles out of Solan, to the hotel, to the walks, to even this guest house, he had tried to recreate the magic that he had once felt with Anita. Anita of the ethereal white kurtas, of the heartbreaking story that had drawn him ineluctably to her, of the violent mood swings that had quickly taxed his love and finally driven him away from her, irretrievably away. Just two years after that honeymoon in Shimla, when he had showered her with his emotions and his passions, his thoughts and his dreams. There had been a certain freshness about it all, then; everything they had seen had been imbued with rainbow colours, sprinkled with gold dust.

When he finally opened his eyes, Shekhar saw that Ranjana was sitting on the stone steps that led down from the veranda. Her head was on her knees. He knew she was crying. He got up, sat next to her and put an arm around her shoulder. She stiffened but did not move away. The light was fading quickly as they sat, together yet separated, as the past is from the present, as yesterday is from today. And as they sat, they also waited, separately, for the presence of a third to fade, fade like the dying light.

She spoke, finally, in a soft whisper.

'Why did you do it?'

Shekhar could not tell her that he had been compelled to complete a script that had been left halfway when the main character had simply disappeared. That the empty stage, the backdrop of mountains and clouds had been waiting for Ranjana to walk in, for the lights to come on, for the action to begin.

Instead, he said: 'I just wanted to do the things that had made me happy, given me joy.'

'But that didn't last. Do you want us to end the same way?'

'I refuse to believe that all happy beginnings end badly. I want to believe in happy beginnings.'

Shekhar got up to pick up the wine glasses and they sat in silence on the stone steps until the chowkidar came out carrying the food.

'May we stay here tonight?' Shekhar asked the chowkidar.

'No, sahib, it is not allowed nowadays.'

'Why, it used to be when I was here the last time.'

'No longer, sahib, leopard attacks.'

Shekhar turned to Ranjana. Instead of the disappointment that he expected, he saw the beginnings of a smile.

'I'm afraid we have to go back to Mount View Hotel,' he continued.

'Only to check out,' Ranjana replied. 'Then we are going to Mashobra. I want to see a different sunrise. There is a nice place I know there. I've been there before.'

Evening at the Club

O ut of sheer habit, the Doctor glanced at his watch as he entered the club. Five past six. Good. The club opened at six and he liked to reach it by five past six. He liked to be the first one there and watch it slowly come to life.

The club boy, Raghu, was switching on the lights.

'Ah, Raghu, what's happening?'

'Nothing, Doctor, you know that nothing ever happens here.'

Raghu was nineteen and wanted to get away from this little mountain ridge, which cut the evening into two with its sharp edges. Raghu hated it because nothing ever happened there, and only four buses passed through it daily.

The Doctor chuckled and watched the boy set out the card tables. I bet he puts the new pack on the corner table, he thought and then smiled sardonically to himself when he was proved right. The Deputy Commissioner and the Superintendent of Police would play on the corner table and they would not like frayed cards. Everything on that table would be fresh and crisp. The cards, the conversation, the scores on the scribble pad and the saris of their wives. Like the white seat covers of their cars that would wait outside. All else, the Doctor looked around, was frayed. The carpets, the chairs, the faces and the hillside.

'Does anybody ever win anything in this game?' The Doctor stylishly threw a magazine on the round table.

Raghu smiled and said nothing. He knew what the Doctor thought of cards.

Slowly and leisurely, the Doctor moved into the billiards room and carefully hung up his blue blazer. Under that he wore a yellow pullover over his grey trousers. His woollen tie had a neat, small check. The Doctor liked to dress for the club, 'though I know it's not the Willingdon, you know, but a club, any club, must have some basic rules.'

At least the billiards room had some rules. The two bank clerks whom the Doctor was currently introducing to the nuances of the game were always well, or at least neatly, turned out. The Doctor would smile to himself as he saw them gradually and unknowingly give in to the addiction of the game. They were already forgetting that it was a strange and mysterious game and were beginning to find meaning in the angles and a certain symmetry on the green baize.

So they were always neatly turned out. Even on Sundays, when Raghu would get mugs of chilled beer and set them out one by one on the window sill. These mugs would settle the score between the Doctor and the clerks that had been chalked up during the week. The Doctor rarely had to pay but he would always buy the last round and leave a generous tip for the boy. And everybody let him because they thought that the old bachelor could afford it.

He began to make easy strokes on the table. The low light threw the edges of the room into shadows, almost hiding the high wooden benches, the cue stand and the tall cupboard with its large mirror. Nobody watched the game and the benches were hardly ever used.

The bank clerks came in unobtrusively and selected their cues.

'So who is going to lose first?' asked the Doctor as he watched them carefully chalk up their cues.

The clerks smiled. They liked to feel like sacrificial lambs before the Doctor's cue and his dry wit. Somehow that made them feel sophisticated. Better than the card players and more manly than the ping-pong kids in the hall.

'Okay, I'll play you both together for a bottle of beer to the first hundred.'

When the game began the shadows seemed to lengthen inwards, creeping unseen towards the rounded and carved legs of the old table.

Everything seemed to concentrate on the rectangle of light where one red and two white balls moved—smoothly when the Doctor pushed them in clean long strokes, and more jerkily when the bank clerks tried to catch up. The balls spun, made delicate impossible angles and were potted. There was nothing that could not be done and nothing else seemed to matter. Outside the window the sun had set behind the third range of low hills that could be seen, and a chilly winter darkness was settling on the town. The peanut seller outside the gates of the club warmed his hand over the little fire that burned in a small earthen pot atop his small mound of peanuts, and the air smelt of the smoke which came from this pot and all the kitchen fires that were now burning. The boys' school was deserted and dark. In the cottage just beyond the school, the Doctor's forty-one-year-old sister sat, sipping tea and talking in gentle tones with Mr Shukla, who taught history at the school.

Mr Shukla leaned back in his chair and drew his shawl around his neck. A cold draught came in through a chink in the window, but he always sat there when he came to see Shanti. He had taken to coming there thrice a week, in the evenings.

'It's getting cold,' Shanti was saying, 'would you like some more tea?'

'No, no, thank you.' Mr Shukla was a careful man. Not too much tea, no coffee and a few words. His words became even fewer when the Doctor was around. He still didn't know how to handle the Doctor's digs about history—'Still teaching the boys about the Emperor and his leather coins?' But with Shanti it was different. She listened to him.

The instrumental music came to an end and Shanti got up to change the side. The records lay neatly stacked near her brother's books. Soon she must cook dinner, but for once she was being lazy. Her brother would not have believed that. 'A washing-ironing-cooking machine', he used to call her, 'a three-in-one'. But she was used to him and his ways. Like the way he, normally a late sleeper, would one day get up much before dawn and go for a run, 'just to break the habit.' Or talk incessantly whenever he had a fever. She was used to all this, and except for the time that he had been in medical college, they had been together.

'Why don't you stay and have some food? Doctor should be home soon, I think.'

'You think I should stay?'

Shanti smiled and nodded. The music began again and drifted down the hillside over the fallen young pines, uprooted just a few days before, in a vicious hailstorm.

'Gently, gently, or you'll pull out the cloth. One smooth motion to the top of the ball, more side.'

The Doctor was demonstrating strokes; the game had long been given up. In the card room, too, the game was about to finish. The Doctor noted this with a peep between the curtains, and timed his entry.

'Hullo, Commissioner.'

The young Deputy Commissioner smiled, knowing that he had years to go before he could drop the 'Deputy'.

'Hullo, Doctor. On billiards as usual.'

The police officer was a gruff man, silent by habit. He waved briefly and returned to his cards. He stared at them intently as if he were comparing a criminal's face with a sketch made from an eyewitness' description.

The Doctor stood around them and watched for a few minutes. That was the only time he had anything to do with the other senior district officials. Except, of course, when they came to him as patients. Or when he got files from the Deputy Commissioner's office. He would go through these files in his small office at the end of the hospital corridor and record his views in neat black ink. There was much talk of a new wing in the hospital, a few extra beds, a mobile clinic. The plan was to name the wing after a former prince of the district with the yet unexpressed hope that his estate would send in a large donation. After he had finished with the files, they would be wrapped up again in a thick green cloth and a peon would carry them on his shoulder down the hill to the Deputy Commissioner's office.

He hardly ever went to their houses. Somehow Shanti was never comfortable there and he did not like to leave her alone after his evenings at the club. That was their special time together, the time after their early dinner. They hardly met during the day so they both looked forward to that hour or two, exchanging a few words, or simply sitting in comfortable silence. During the summer they would sit in the veranda on the rounded cane chairs watching the lights in the valley. In the winters they would warm themselves by the fireside drinking mugs of light tea and he would usually drift away to sleep with a book in his hands.

The Doctor excused himself and went back to the bank clerks. 'Another round of fifty?'

'No, Doctor, I have to go before they close the bread shop.'

'Eat cake. Oh, nothing, forget it.'

'And I, too, must move. Some homework with the kids. This new math is simply beyond me.'

'Okay, so you two won't stay. But remember—all that matters is practice. Colonel Jai couldn't hit a cannon at six inches when he first came, but the way he practised!'

Guiltily the bank clerks moved away. Raghu was waiting with the chain for the gate in his hand. The Doctor waved to him and started up the hill with his long loping stride. The last bus was coming up from the valley. It puffed and steamed, threatening to come to a halt after each incline. But somehow it carried on, each painful bend in its progress celebrated with a long honk. He looked over the valley once, before he ambled up the path that finally led to the cottage. When he sat down for dinner with Shanti and Mr Shukla, he was still thinking of the river that lay in the darkness of the valley, where he used to go fishing so regularly until one day he just gave it up. While they ate they could hear the bus reach the final curve, and with one last triumphant honk, it clattered to a stop. In the cold night, they could hear the shouts of the passengers as they climbed out and the scraping of the metal boxes as they slid down the ladder. Then there was silence and they had their tea. And Mr Shukla told the Doctor that he and Shanti wanted to get married.

The simple ceremony was performed in the little white marble temple at the edge of the hill. It was attended by a few junior doctors, some students and the two bank clerks. The Deputy Commissioner and the Superintendent of Police came together in one car just in time to congratulate the couple.

That day the Doctor gave the club a miss. And after that Raghu stopped expecting him at five past six every day, and was no longer sure of his Sunday tip.

A Saturday Lunch

I had known Alex when she was twenty-three or so and we both lived in the romantic land of churches and castles, wide open plains and the broad, slow moving river. But an image of her had remained with me these five or six years in some sunlit recess of my mind, shut away from the everyday clutter. In that image I remembered her as I had last seen her. I had stopped my car at a pedestrian crossing and she had stepped across the road lightly, a slim, flaxen-haired girl with a face almost as white as chalk. She had not seen me, and such had been the momentary charm of that image heightened by the sombre beauty of a dark church in the background that I had not called out. And then the traffic had pushed us apart.

That image had hung over the telephone conversation we'd had in this new, clean, antiseptic town, where I had discovered her accidentally. She remembered me quite well—and in fact we must get together for lunch. In fact, why not Saturday? One-thirty? I accepted, though it bothered me that she was willing to host a lunch on a weekend for someone she hadn't met in years. And besides that, I did not know her husband at all. All I knew about him, and I am afraid I don't quite remember now how I came to know it, was that he was much older than she, at least twenty years older. There was no other option but to accept the invitation. It seemed the only way to satisfy my curiosity.

Saturday was a cold, blustery day, the kind of day I have begun to like as I've grown older. Such days give me a perfect excuse for not going out. A strong wind rose from the lake and swept across the valley. Low, grey clouds hid the mountaintops, which I was sure had a hint of snow already even though it was early October. I felt strangely stupid, standing in the wind outside the low straggling house with a little garden, carrying a bouquet of red flowers. They were rather large, red flowers, with long tongues. Quite artistic, I thought, though I now forget its French name. When the door opened and Alex greeted me with a warm and genuine smile, I knew that it had been all right. Her look reassured me that it had been the right decision to ring her up, to come for lunch and to bring red flowers.

'What lovely flowers! And isn't it wonderful to see you, after so many years?'

There was no hint of polite exaggeration in her voice. She meant it and, spontaneously, she raised her chin so that I could greet her with a kiss. I have never been too good at this sort of thing and I found myself fumbling with her proximity and her perfume and, awkwardly, I kissed the air near her cheeks wondering why this had to be done thrice or, for that matter, at all.

'Meet Michael,' she said, leading me by the hand to her husband.

He had been standing a little away, a glass of campari and tonic in his hand, waiting for us to finish our greeting as it were. Now he came forward and held out a very white, thin hand.

'Glad to meet you. Alex has spoken of you very often.'

He led me through a little alcove into a wide sitting room while Alex hurried away in what I presumed was the direction of the kitchen, her pointed heels making thin sounds on the wooden floor.

'She'll be back,' he said without even looking at me. 'It's the cake that is still in the oven.'

It was a cozy and comfortable room holding its own against the cold afternoon outside. The chairs were large and brown and soft with matching broad cushions. A study angled out of the room where I could see book-lined shelves and the side of a huge black music speaker. Rich rugs from Central Asia and Afghanistan hung from a wooden railing into the room and there were dark paintings on the walls. They all seemed to have been done by the same artist. All of them had thin, angular faces and broad tree trunks and somehow reminded one of the broad plains and rivers and forests of Russia. I looked around and went to peer closely at one of the paintings.

'An unknown Romanian artist. We bought them cheap in New York. But who knows, he might be famous one day... Anyhow, we may as well sit down. Where would you like to sit?'

I found it a somewhat odd question and made to move towards a large comfortable looking sofa. Immediately a huge grey cat leapt from behind me and perched itself on the arm of the sofa. It glared at me with its yellow-green eyes, its fur bristled and its tail stiff.

'Yes, I'm sorry,' said Michael. 'I'm afraid Mitch will not let you sit on that one. That's my chair. I sit there in the mornings usually and watch the garden with Mitch, since I have nothing much to do otherwise.'

I turned and sat down in the other chair while Michael took his seat. The cat calmed down and curled up comfortably near him. He made a perfect picture, slouched deep into the sofa, his shoulders hunched forward, his white bony hands gently turning the glass around feeling the texture of its rim with an occasional swish of the finger. I could imagine him sitting like that day after day, the large cat curled up on the arm of the sofa, contemplating the mysteries of the terraced, very green garden as Alex went about her business in town. He fitted in perfectly against the dark painting on the wall behind him, and for a moment I thought that he was part of the painting.

Alex returned, drying her hands. Her smile immediately lightened the room, and Michael and the cat lost their sombreness and began to look very normal, just an old man and his cat. She came and sat near me and we began to talk. We traced out the years and tried to fill in the gaps since we had last met. Michael listened quietly until our conversation reached a natural point where he could be drawn in. Alex looked at him fondly as she began to talk about their recent holiday in Venice. It had been a brief but wonderful holiday. They had rented an apartment in Jesolo almost fifty kilometres outside the city, from where they used to drive to the city on thin ribs of land.

'It's such a wonderful, romantic city,' said Alex, 'timeless, you know. When you stand on one of those arched bridges over the canals, you could be in any century. And Michael loved it so much, didn't you, dear?'

She again enveloped her husband in a warm, embracing look. And at last he seemed to bring himself to respond, goaded on by that look.

'Actually, what I liked best was the restaurant we discovered. We discovered it quite by accident, you know. We were caught in a shower without umbrellas. And there was this little door which led into a sort of quadrangle where we found this large, friendly, warm restaurant. It was not the food really, but the champagne that took us there every day after that.

'Wasn't it romantic, Michael? To have pink champagne at eleven in the morning. I mean, in Venice one can do these things without feeling the slightest guilt.' Alex's voice was languorous now. 'And they serve it in those really thin flute glasses. God, Michael, can't I have some now?'

Michael pulled himself out of the sofa reluctantly and I could almost hear the groan straining on his lips. He went into the kitchen silently and in a few moments came back with three very thin flute glasses of chilled pink champagne on a tray.

'Yes,' he said before I could make any observation, 'we even bought these glasses there because Alex was convinced that the champagne would not have tasted the same in any other glass. Perhaps she's right.'

Then we gave ourselves up to the ceremony of sipping the pink champagne as the cold wind blew outside. I got the feeling that they would have done the same even if I had not been around. The champagne was good and I could well imagine its temptation in Venice or out of Venice. The ceremony ended abruptly as a sudden gust of wind banged shut some window in the house and large drops of rain splattered the glass doors that looked out into the garden. It seemed to be the cue for us to move to the table.

'We can carry on with our champagne at the table,' said Michael, 'though I had rather looked forward to starting with the white wine.'

We sat down at the carefully laid table. It had been set for three in such a manner that we did not miss a fourth person. From where I sat I could watch a patch of the lawn and the fine drizzle that slanted on to it. It gave me a strangely comfortable feeling and reminded me of the green, wet hillsides of my youth.

Alex then began to talk with enthusiasm about her work and how she enjoyed it thoroughly. She was running the cultural centre at the embassy and that meant meeting a lot of interesting, talented people. It meant a lot of socializing, partying and even some travel. Just last month she had been on official business to Hungary.

'You cannot imagine Budapest. Have you ever been there?' She leaned towards me as she spoke and I remembered how her eyes had always been so intensely blue.

'No.'

'Then I cannot possibly explain to you the sheer beauty and charm of that city. It is ex-qui-site.'

Michael appeared to have gone into some private shell. At last he spoke—'Are you sure we should be having champagne with this fish?'

'Yes dear, I think it's fine,' Alex cut in smoothly.

'Are you quite sure, I mean? Somehow it does not seem to be the correct thing to do. I think we should be really having the white wine I have chilled all morning.'

'Of course dear, we can still have the wine. Would you like some white wine?'

The question seemed to be lying on my plate for a lifetime and I watched it, hesitating to pass a judgement. But this time it was Michael who cut in quickly.

'That's not fair, not fair at all. How can he now have white wine when we're nearly through with the first course on pink champagne? It's not even fair to ask.'

'It's really quite fine,' I said and I thought that was a fairly neutral answer. My mind searched around wildly for something to say that would change the subject without seeming to. I didn't want to talk of the weather for fear of pushing Michael further down the black mood that seemed to be enveloping him. But he seemed to have read my mind.

'Oh God, this weather,' his voice was almost a vicious whisper, 'they say it comes from the north. That's not true. It's the change that's coming over the entire world. You can't say anything with any reasonable certainty about the weather anymore.'

I stole a glance at Alex. Her white face was pinched and bleak and she was staring at her plate. But in a minute she was all enthusiasm again, gathering up the plates and rushing into the kitchen to get the main course. She came back with plates of roast mutton cuts with beans and small round potatoes.

'I hope it's not overdone for you,' Michael enquired as we started eating. 'You know, there is no meat worse than overdone roast lamb. Alex does tend to overdo it sometimes.'

'It's excellent,' I responded, surprised at my own alacrity in rising to Alex's defence.

We ate on in silence until we reached a point where someone simply had to speak. It was Alex.

'You must talk to Michael about his book. You know he's working on one. I mentioned it that day when we spoke on the phone.'

I did not recall her having mentioned it but such was the persuasion in her voice that I nodded readily. I felt that we were launching an exciting conspiracy against the old man. In any case I should not have been surprised that he was writing a book. Just about anybody I had met in the last year or so had been writing a book.

'How is it going?' I asked. 'I mean, how much more work do you have left on it?'

Michael's face grimaced in mock horror.

'Oh, are we now going to talk of my painful mornings just when I'm beginning to enjoy the lunch? This is not fair.'

Nevertheless he began to talk about the book. It was a book about what he had done all his life—teaching at a university. It was part autobiographical, part analytical. I imagined a mix of university politics, anecdotes and paragraphs on the ills attending the educational system. Then suddenly, he broke off and changed the subject.

'This wine has been one big, awful mistake. We are now continuing to have white wine when we should have been having red.'

He shot an accusing glance at his wife, who kept silent. In fact, after that we all kept silent through the lunch. The awkwardness of the silence seemed less troublesome than what could have been started off by any remark about the food or the wine or the weather. Mercifully, the silence was broken by the cat that had gone into the garden through some open window and now scratched the garden door in the dining room, wanting to be let in. Alex got up and picked her up and then we all moved to the study for coffee.

As we entered the study, Michael seemed to become a different person. For the first time that afternoon I felt that he was comfortable and relaxed. He sank into a sofa with a large black and brown pattern that stood against a wall covered with vaguely sentimental black-and-white photographs, portraits of shadowy friends and relatives, and a somewhat incongruous faded watercolour of an old European town in winter. The smell of fresh coffee went well with the walnut wood writing desk, the shelves full of books and the untidy heap of magazines. Michael seemed to expand with well-being as he lit a cigarette and puffed at it with a passionate relish, letting the smoke leave him reluctantly in a thin whistle from the side of his mouth. Obviously he looked forward to his after-lunch cigarette.

'I have actually left smoking, except for this one cigarette a day.'

'How do you feel about it?' I asked, keen to make him talk.

'Oh, I feel a changed man. I am miserable.'

We laughed and I watched fascinated as his pinched face dissolved in good-natured wrinkles. His bushy eyebrows were no longer severe but comic, and his cold piercing blue eyes were filmed with moisture. The years fell away from his face and he was obviously enjoying himself. He talked with an incisiveness that had been absent in the earlier afternoon. He talked mostly of the past, of men he had known and the countries to which he had travelled. He talked passionately, like a man who, at late afternoon, cannot forget how bright and hot the sun had been at midday.

When the conversation seemed to have run out of steam I made a move to go. Immediately Michael's face darkened and he regained his pinched expression.

'Is he going away now?' he said aloud, almost to no one.

'Yes, I really must,' I replied.

I shook hands with him in the study. Alex saw me off to the door and held up her face for me to kiss as she had when I had come. I remember leaving the house with strangely confused feelings.

A couple of weeks later I saw Alex again. Once again it was a traffic junction but this time she wasn't walking. She was in a car that drove past me. It was a green, expensive sports car with the hood down. Her flaxen hair streamed behind her and her white tennis dress reflected the afternoon sun. A young man in a white tennis shirt, open at the neck, was driving the car. Both of them were laughing. Alex's face was radiant and her eyes shone, reminding me of the time that I had been in love. I don't think she saw me.

On Official Duty

Mr Krishnan was a senior officer in the government. Everything about him testified to the fact. He was neat and tidy. He was meticulous and organized. He was careful with his words and his money. He was deliberate and restrained, almost slow in his reactions. It did not matter whether the question was about the next major change in the country's environment policy or simply about the best flight to take to Geneva. His mind, trained through thirty-three years of a demanding bureaucratic career, would go through the automatic process of weighing the pros against the cons, and the decision, mature and well-considered, would eventually present itself.

As their plane touched down at the small, neat and picturesque Cointrin Airport at Geneva, the two younger officers travelling with Mr Krishnan silently admired his decision to take this particular flight. It had brought them in just after lunch. That left the entire summer afternoon and evening free. The meeting was only scheduled to begin the next day. They would be able to look around the city, go for a walk around the famous lake, and perhaps even finish off the obligatory shopping for chocolates and cheese. Mr Krishnan's experienced paperwork had even ensured that much of the Saturday after the meeting in Geneva would be spent attending ostensibly to 'further consultations'. These would surely not last the whole day and would leave them some more time to take in the sights. It was clear to them that being with a man like him was a good thing and they had done well to endear themselves to him.

At the conveyor belt, he talked to them in gentle measured tones while waiting for the baggage. The official from the embassy who had been detailed to receive them went in search of a baggage trolley. Mr Krishnan was always inwardly tense about his baggage. But he thought it a weakness to show it and preferred to keep up a brave front.

'It always arrives, you must have faith in that,' he told the younger officers. 'In ninety-nine point nine cases, it will turn up. When you travel a lot you have to develop a faith in the system, otherwise you become like Ganguly. He is so paranoid that he is worried about his baggage even when he is touring by car. He stops the car at least once every hundred kilometres and checks if his suitcase is in the boot.'

The young officers smiled at the story. They had, of course, heard it before. But Mr Krishnan did not tell them that despite his faith in the system, he always carried all his valuables and an emergency set —a shirt, trousers and tie—in the burgundy-coloured leather satchel in his hand. This satchel had been his faithful companion on many journeys abroad. It was an old satchel—the leather had developed cracks and the golden buttons had long lost their shine. But he did not want to part with it simply because it could stretch effortlessly to hold this emergency kit in addition to his official papers.

At the hotel Mr Krishnan was quick and efficient with the embassy official. It was another of his self-imposed rules to never complain about the hotel rooms that the embassies selected. He had noticed other officers demand lake-facing rooms or rooms with a balcony, and to him that had seemed petty. He regarded a hotel room as a mere space of transit in which one had to sleep for a night or two. This one was as good as any other. It had a decent bed, a sofa set, a writing desk with a stationery pad, a bowl of fruit and, no doubt, it had a perfectly functional washroom.

He took the blue folder that the official was carrying. It contained a neat white envelope with his allowance. Mr Krishnan glanced at the money and put it into his inner coat pocket. Then he signed the three copies of the voucher and handed back two, keeping one for his record. The folder also contained a list of telephone numbers, a country note with tips for visitors and a map of Geneva. There was also an invitation card for a dinner at the house of one of the officers. He kept the folder near the telephone on the bedside table. The formalities done, the official left, grateful that he had not been asked to stay on and assist with the shopping.

But that was not Mr Krishnan's style. He had come to work, and work was uppermost in his mind. He promptly unpacked, and hung up the navy blue and the grey pinstriped suits that he had brought in the cupboard, noting that they had got slightly crushed at the shoulders. He put the four white shirts in a neat pile on the shelf and settled his ties and socks in the chest of drawers. Then he had a quick wash and changed into a comfortable brown cardigan and pistachio green slacks and was ready to receive his two younger colleagues. Although they had the whole afternoon before them he liked to get this over with.

They sat on the sofa, sipped orange juice and went through the agenda of the meeting. Right away, Mr Krishnan began to efficiently outline the strategy for the delegation, and divided the work. He told them what to say and how to say it and declared the bottom lines that they had in the negotiations. He indicated to them that they would have to stick to those bottom lines. He kept the fallback positions to himself. If the need for any flexibility arose, he would intervene himself as and when he deemed fit. Then the two younger officers left, secure in the knowledge that he would not need them for the rest of the day.

He swept aside the curtain and stepped on to the little balcony outside his room. He leaned on the carved iron railing and took in the view. It was a late April afternoon, sunny and bright. The lake was an iridescent blue and the famous Geneva fountain showered its white spray into the deep blue sky. Colourful flags lined the famous bridge across the lake. The old town rose above the lake and was topped off by the spire of the imposing cathedral. Behind it all, he could see clearly the shoulder of Mont Blanc with its eternal snow. It was a day to walk.

Making a quick decision, he stepped back into the room and shut the door. He changed into a pair of soft black corduroy walking shoes without which he never left his house. He had discovered these shoes during one of his early postings in a small hill-district capital and found them ideal for walking. Since then he had regularly bought a pair once every two years. He put on a spring overcoat that he had wisely packed in after having watched the weather forecasts on satellite TV before leaving. He did not have a cap, he thought, as he looked into the full-length mirror. He ran a hand tentatively over his head, which was balding in the centre. The silver growth which framed the bald patch was allowed to grow an extra half inch in length as if to make up for it. The navy blue spring overcoat did not quite match with the brown cardigan, pistachio green slacks and black corduroy shoes. But such things had not mattered to Mr Krishnan for years. He was a man concerned only with essentials, and the essential thing was to walk and not catch a cold in the process.

As he stepped on to the promenade by the lake, he buttoned his coat up to his collar and put his hands into his pockets. Then he began to walk fast in order to get his regular exercise. He was used to walking regularly every morning in the Lodhi Gardens in Delhi. In fact he was so regular every morning that his wife timed herself just listening to him. At six-thirty he would leave for his walk. At five past seven he would return and would sit down with his tea and the newspaper. Halfway through the newspaper, seven-fifteen that is, he would say—'I'll give one hundred rupees to anyone who says that I don't need to go to office today.' No matter what the newspaper said about inflation, the hundred rupees never changed. At seven-thirty it was always—'Why can't I ever find my comb?' And it would be approximately ten past eight when he would say—'I say I am getting late and today there are very important meetings.' He had missed his morning walk that day and intended to make up for it. So he walked briskly and purposefully, scarcely glancing at the shop displays, having decided years ago that nothing, except perhaps medicines, should be bought abroad.

But it was difficult to walk fast along the low wall that bounded the lake. There were youngsters twirling in merriment on rollerblades, there were toddlers clutching colourful ice creams, there were lovers holding on to eternity on the benches, there were white sails flitting on the blue water, and incredible clouds wafting overhead. A sense of freedom suffused the air and carelessness was flung like a magic carpet over the summer afternoon. Mr Krishnan felt this spirit overpowering him. For a moment he resisted and then, without quite knowing when, he had become a part of it. He slackened his pace, his arms relaxed and his face softened. The lake became a deeper blue as he gazed on it, and a sharp sense of beauty impressed itself upon him. He leaned against the promenade wall as if drawing strength from it. A man, his light blue shirt open to the waist and a cigarette dangling from his lips, was standing on a high stepladder and carving a larger-than-life stone statue of an embracing couple. Mr Krishnan watched him as he made sharp jabs with his chisel to evoke a shoulder muscle out of stone. In fact he watched him for a long time and was lost in the man's efforts to make the stone surrender its primordial form.

Then a familiar yet long forgotten smell caught him unawares. It was the smell of hot chocolate sauce on fresh crêpes from the stall near him. In an instant it took him back years. Almost a lifetime. To a week he had spent in Paris. He was a student on his way back from London with his university degree. For a week he had tramped around Montmartre, and had eaten crêpes with hot chocolate sauce every day at the little shop in the corner of the famous artists' square. It had all been so new, so magical. It had been the beginning of things. Everything, even the fresh crêpes, had been a grand adventure. For a week he had wallowed in that adventure, watching the artists with their instant portraits, dabbing paint on canvases, cutting fascinating profiles of passers-by out of black paper, and playing flutes and violins. He had absorbed the music that flew out of the twilight bars. He had sat on the wide steps below the huge cathedral, a can of beer in his hand, and watched the grey beauty of the Parisian sky. He had made friends, laughed spontaneously and perhaps, for a moment or two, even felt the stirrings of passion. Then he had tucked away that week under piles of discipline, folded it away in swathes of regularity, and tied up the whole package with the suffocating ribbon of duty. Much had been achieved in the years that followed. There had been success, security, recognition and even love, for Mr Krishnan had performed all his roles with distinction and aplomb. And now he was only a year and a half away from retirement, the moment of release that would also take away in its wake so much that had become so important.

He looked up to see that the lights had come on in the windows of the hotels that lined the lakefront. The traffic had increased. It was time for people to return home from work. Three decades had gone like that, just going to work and coming back. And yet, that week in Paris haunted him still.

Deep inside him, Mr Krishnan felt a long lost beckoning. His disciplined, regular mind went through the pros and cons and the decision presented itself. Then he went back to the hotel and changed into the grey pinstriped suit that he had hung in the cupboard earlier in the day. He changed the comfortable walking shoes for the formal leather pair. He carefully counted the amount of money in the neat white envelope and put it in his pocket. After a momentary hesitation, he left behind the spring overcoat. He wouldn't be walking tonight. The concierge in the hotel lobby handed him a brochure and ordered a cab. It took him only twenty minutes to reach Divonne.

Divonne is a small French village that borders Geneva. It is tucked under a mountain and has a well-known chateau and a small lake. With a lively fresh market on Sundays and a decent golf course, it also has a casino.

Mr Krishnan entered the casino with quiet authority and confidence. A hostess wearing a black backless dress guided him inside. He mused over the bar and finally ordered a single malt whisky on the rocks. He walked through the casino holding his glass, sipping very occasionally, feeling the tiny smoky drops slowly warm his insides. He picked up a bundle of coins at the change counter and decided to try his luck at the slot machines.

There was an old lady at the machine next to him, and he

watched her discreetly for a few minutes. Neck bowed down with necklaces, hands trembling slightly, she played the machine relentlessly and without a minute's break. Her winnings kept racing upwards on the counter. Then, with a final swish, she encashed them all and let the coins flow in a metallic rush into the out tray. Mr Krishnan followed her example and sensed exhilaration rising in his veins. After a while, tired of the loneliness of the machine, he joined one of the green tables with three others and let himself go. He played tenaciously through the night. He tried every game that the house had to offer. He refilled his glass at the bar several times. He laughed, he joked and he jibed. In a generous gesture, he even bought a round of drinks for the group of young executives and fashion models that he joined for part of the night. When he finally left the casino, it was still dark. But the dawn was not long in coming.

At fifteen past nine in the morning, the two young officers knocked respectfully at Mr Krishnan's door. They had slept well after an inexpensive meal for dinner and a stroll around the lake. They had debated for a while whether or not to go for a show in one of the restaurants and then, on considerations of economy and health, had dropped the idea.

He was waiting for them. As they came in, he picked up his papers from the table and arranged them neatly into his briefcase. The white envelope that had contained his allowance, still uncreased, was empty and he tossed it gently into the waste-paper basket. Just once, before leaving the room, he felt the bundle of folded and adventurous notes that lay in his inner pocket, and smiled. He was ready for the negotiations.

A Golden Twilight

Mrs Lal had to accompany her son to all the dinners that were hosted in his honour. She knew it was important for the local officials to make a good first impression on the district collector and there was no way that they would agree to leave her out. Nevertheless, she did find it repetitive. The talk would mostly be official and the ladies would let the men have a free hand so that they could make the right impact. There would also be almost the same menu in each house, spiced with the daily dose of discreet gossip, just enough to make the collector feel that he had come to an interesting place, not just another small town.

She could feel the wives observing her, polite but unsure. They would have been more comfortable with a wife than a mother. They would have taken her to the club or vied with each other to take her on that first and most important shopping trip. Then they would have let her know somewhat half-heartedly what really happened to the last collector and what awful taste his wife had. But with Mrs Lal they remained distant and polite, confining themselves to household tips.

'The fresh butter comes by the seven o'clock bus. You should get it from the corner bakery. Or you could send the servant, of course.'

'And the vegetables, best to tell them to deliver them home. They will do it for you, they must.'

But the first week was soon over and with the pressure of the dinners behind them, the ladies delivered their verdicts on her at the club. The eleven o'clock coffee session had been resumed and was full of the new arrival.

'I mean, did she really have to come to all those dinners, at her age?' asked the corpulent wife of the chief engineer, halfway through an oily chicken roll.

'At least sixty-five, I think,' said a twenty-five-year-old new wife. 'Or maybe...seventy?'

'What plain saris! Fine for her age, maybe.' This came from the woman whose sister ran a fashion boutique in Delhi.

'And the way she looks away when you are talking to her and begins to stare out of the window, I tell you, most irritating.'

At this point they called for a second round of coffee and carried on. Mrs Lal, of course, never came to the club.

The baggage soon arrived in huge wooden crates in a truck which had invocations to the Hill Goddess painted on its bumper. The large and sprawling bungalow quickly swallowed up the crates, and Mrs Lal began slowly to bring it to life. When the books were all finally arranged in the study and the crockery was systematically set in the sideboards in the dining room, Mrs Lal taught the servants how to clean and dust. They learnt soon what time to bring the bed tea and how much salt to add to the food. And when they came back from the daily shopping trips, they gave her an account of the expenditure on narrow strips of paper, which the local shopkeepers used. One room in the front section of the bungalow was turned into an office, for the collector inevitably brought home bundles of files, and people from the villages in the interior came to see him in the evenings and on the weekends.

When she finally found the time to wander into the town, she avoided the straggling bazaar that went down to the small railway station. Instead she began to frequent the town library. It was a long, dusty library which seemed to be housed in a corridor rather than a hall, and in which a few old men were perpetually reading newspapers. The books that she borrowed hadn't been borrowed for a long time. The last entries had been made in black angled handwriting with an old-fashioned, thick-nibbed pen. The ink was fading and the yellowing pages seemed to smell of talcum powder. The librarian liked her because she had begun to borrow those forgotten books, and told her longingly of the days when the library had been the centre of the town.

In the evenings she took to going for long walks. Her favourite walk would take her down Circular Road, where it left the vegetable shops and curved in a long languorous loop around Pine Hill. It was a quiet and lonely road. There were hardly any houses, and the occasional cottage lay either far below or far above the road. For the first half of the loop she had an almost uninterrupted view of the valley, and far away in it she could see the ruins of an old brewery. And just at the end of the loop, when it seemed to be stretched out in such tension that it would surely have gone off at a tangent over the twilit valleys had it not turned back just then, she would come to a cemetery. It was an old cemetery, not used since the days of the Englishmen, and there was a crumbling stone bench above it. Here, Mrs Lal would sit and watch the sunset.

She loved the fresh smell that came from the pines which stood out straight on the scrambling slope, and she loved the way the dusk seemed to linger in the valley till the last possible minute, before settling down unobtrusively into every turn and twist. It reminded her of the early morning walks in Delhi forty years ago. It was probably the moist feeling that touched off the memory. The grass used to be wet with dew, and she had loved to walk barefoot on the lawns between the twin canals in the centre of Delhi.

That fresh early morning feeling was all she wanted to remember of the hot and bloody summer in which she, her husband and their two small children had formed a hopeless molecule in the terrible upheaval that had convulsed the country. It had been a summer of plunder and loot, madness and murder. They had come to Delhi, holding on to life without any real hope. Pushed on helplessly, they had been allotted a room in the hutments which had housed wartime British offices. Each family had a room, there was a common bathroom, and all the children played together in the hollow square. The children had begun to play even then and that had perhaps been the best way to rebuild life. For, in any case, there had been no logic to anything and there were no answers, only the compulsive need to go on.

It was in those days that she had been plagued by such a deep restlessness that it would often keep her awake at night. At sunrise, she would walk the three kilometres to the wet grass lawns at India Gate to give play to the restlessness, searching somewhere within for the strength for the day ahead.

The same restlessness became a part of her walks down Circular Road. Her mind would be in turmoil and the years would go back and forth, cutting across tragedies and suddenly brightening up with glimpses of happiness. It would all begin to come back with a blazing intensity, leaving a high colour on her face by the time she returned from the walk.

The walk became an addiction and she began to look forward to it with an anticipation she hadn't felt for anything at all in years. Each day she would select for herself a phase of her life, a decade or a moment, and give herself up to it completely. And it would reward her with a flood of emotions and memories and feelings, as if in a torrent of gratitude, just for being recalled again. A girl, her hair in twin braids, skipping to school in a distant town; a youthful face which seemed a musty photograph even to herself; or the empty dullness of the plateau that had come after that. It all came and went, searing her consciousness and leaving her drained and exhausted.

Sitting on the old bench over the cemetery one evening, she thought a long time about her husband. She didn't think of his weak ambition or his pathetic failures, but of his gentle smile, which appeared to give him strength and a kind of majesty even in his poverty. She wouldn't believe even now that he had been an ordinary man who had died a few years ago and gone into the limitless void. He still seemed to be living on like all the moments that wouldn't die within her. As she thought of him, the last light was leaving the tombstones, each with its name and dates, the mark of forgotten soldiers and administrators. Halting overtures to immortality that were doomed even before they were uttered, pathetic pleadings to faithless memory. They too had gone down into the same limitless blue valley, leaving behind verses on stone which sounded momentous and ridiculous at the same time.

In the fading light, a hawk came into her vision like the spirit of life itself. It rose from the depths of the valley and circled upwards, battling the breeze. With a final burst, it rose and was silhouetted for a moment against the sun. Then it broke free of the sun and soared higher, exulting, free. With it her spirit seemed to soar too, for a moment that was an eternity, into the darkening blue above.

And sitting on that bench that night Mrs Lal wrote her first poem in forty years, on the back of an envelope.

She wrote every day after that. The poems, according to the critic who reviewed her first book a few months later, were not the poems written by an old person. There was a freshness and yearning in them that cried youth. It was all over Mrs Lal's face that would light up with a smile, and which reminded her son of the old forgotten photographs in the family album. He saw the smile, he was a child again and he understood. When he was transferred two years later, he would not force her to go with him. She stayed back, moving into a cottage on Pine Hill.

Author's Note

'The Masterpiece' was first broadcast on the BBC World Service radio in 1988.

'A Certain Thing' was first published in the *London Magazine* in 1989.

'Rumki' was first broadcast on the BBC World Service radio in 1991.

'Evening at the Club' first appeared in the *London Magazine* in 1991.

'A Golden Twilight' was first published in the anthology *Signals: thirty new stories to celebrate thirty years of the 'London Magazine'* in 1991.

'Forgotten Tunes' was first broadcast on the BBC World Service radio in 1994.

'Winter Evenings' first appeared in the *London Magazine* in 1995.

'A Death in Winter' was first published in the *London Magazine* in 1999.

'The Superintendent's Formula' first appeared in the anthology *Signals-2: 25* London Magazine *Stories* in 1999.

'Brute' was first published in *The Statesman* in 2000.

'Delhi' first appeared in *Femina*.

'Madam Kitty' first appeared in *The HarperCollins Book of New Indian Fiction: Contemporary Writing in English* in 2005.

'Sunrise at Mashobra' first appeared in *First Proof: the Penguin Book of New Writings from India* in 2005.

'On Official Duty' was first published in *Himal Southasian* in 2011.

Acknowledgements

A quarter century ago, I mailed three stories in a brown envelope to Alan Ross of the *London Magazine*. A few weeks later, he wrote back asking if he could keep all three and publish them one by one. This generous act and the many years of friendly encouragement that followed kept me going on the uphills of becoming a writer. Thank you Alan; if you had been around today we would have stepped out for a g. and t. and talked cricket.

My warm thanks also to Ravi Singh for his discerning support and guidance for this and other projects and to Aishwarya Iyer for her diligent editing of the stories.

IF I DIE TODAY
Shashi Deshpande

*'It seemed to me that Guru had begun to see himself
as a spectator, above and different from all of us.
That's when a man becomes dangerous: he imagines
himself God and loses touch with humanity.
Whatever Guru's motives may have been,
the results were catastrophic.'*

~

Guru, an end-stage cancer patient, comes to a quiet medical campus
and quickly befriends his host's friends and neighbours, his warmth and
sympathetic manner encouraging them to confide in him. Out of these
conversations emerges a name—Prabhakar Tambe—which spreads a pall
of uneasiness over the doctors and triggers a chain of events that leads
to catastrophic results. Rumours start to fly, old tensions and rivalries
between colleagues and friends resurface, and every family on the
campus is caught in a web of suspicion. Within weeks, two people die
in mysterious circumstances and it seems that life will never be the same
again for the doctors and their families.

A deeply sensitive portrayal of human relationships, *If I Die Today*
is an incisive and compelling picture of murder and what it does
to a community.

A LITTLE BOOK OF LIFE
Ruskin Bond

*'May you have
the wisdom to be simple,
and the humour to be happy!'*

~

Ruskin Bond, India's most loved author, puts together his favourite
sayings, aphorisms and quotations in this delightful little book
on life and living. Drawing on his own observations and life experiences
and those of his favourite authors, he presents thoughts on nature,
friendship, love, family, money, enemies—in short, pithy statements.
This is a book you can dip into anytime, and come up with something
that will make you smile or think with its wit
and gentle common sense.